A SOUND IDEA GONE WRONG

As Lorna disappeared into the house, he stared after her, then turned toward the domed crystal groupings around him and clapped his hands over his ears. I could well imagine what even the desensitized Sirens must be doing to his nerves. Dalriadian took a step toward the nearest bed. He stopped, then without warning, spun and picked up a sculpture in both hands.

"No!" I was too far away for him to hear, but I shouted anyway. "Don't!"

He swung the sculpture like an axe and struck the top of the dome. The habitat had been built to withstand careless handling, but not deliberate assault. It shattered raggedly. Still gripping the sculpture, he turned toward a second bed.

I clutched at the wheel of the truck, steeling myself for what I was powerless to prevent . . .

Also by Lee Killough
Published by Ballantine Books:

DEADLY SILENTS

THE DOPPELGÄNGER GAMBIT

THE MONITOR, THE MINERS AND THE SHREE

A VOICE OUT OF RAMAH

AVENTINE

oooooooooooooooooooooooooooooooooooooo

Lee Killough

A Del Rey Book

BALLANTINE BOOKS • NEW YORK

A Del Rey Book
Published by Ballantine Books

Library of Congress Catalog Card Number: 81-67839

ISBN 0-345-29521-8

Manufactured in the United States of America

First Ballantine Books Edition: January 1982

Cover art by Michael Herring

ACKNOWLEDGMENTS

For PAT, chief critic and cheerleader, and for the many fans who wanted this collection.

Contents

ooooooooooooooooooo

Introduction

○○○○○○○○○○○○○○○○○○○○○○○

WELCOME to Aventine, a mountain community with two lakes: the long, narrow ribbon of the cool, blue Lunamere and, above it, the Heliomere, bath-water warm. Seclusion is guaranteed; the town is accessible only by private aircraft or cabletrain from the nearest neighbor Gateside, whose Diana Mountain stargate and jetport put that city on a crossroads of the galaxy. The original residents were members of an artist's colony; the population has by now expanded to include numerous rich, famous, and often bizarre people seeking a temporary or extended retreat.

In Aventine, everyone is beautiful; cosmetisculpture surgeons guarantee it. Life-style and living quarters are limited only by imagination. Residents may enjoy both TV and holographic symphonies, jets and interstellar travel. Furniture changes color and shape to match the owner's moods, and rather than remaining static, the statuary moves, responding to light, sound, motion, or even nearby personalities. The outside world coexists with a society in which split personalities live without pressure to reassociate and become "normal" and where beautiful women and twisted artists can get away with murder. No one worries about clogged plumbing, energy conservation, or foreign policy.

Aventine is the perfect getaway, the absolute retreat, a dream—a perpetual holiday out of the world and time.

✳   ✳   ✳

The series of stories featuring it began without design, with a story titled "The Siren Garden," but the roots of Aventine sprang from another, older story, "Like Manna," which was not an Aventine story at all. In it, Mars had life, based on silicon, and the waste droppings of one species were smoky red stones coveted as gems by Earthmen. I sent the story to Ejler Jakobsson at *Galaxy,* who sent it back with the comment that while he could not use the present story, he liked the idea of living gems and if I should ever happen to write about *them,* he would like to see the story.

I am nothing if not willing to try pleasing editors, and over the next few years, plots with living gems rolled out of my typewriter. For a long time, however, none ever managed to become more than unfinished rough drafts, not until my living gems met Vermilion Sands.

The creative process, the source of story ideas, is similar to producing recombinant DNA, I think. Bits and pieces of everything a writer sees and hears and reads drop into the stew of his subconscious, where they float, bumping together in varying combinations until a critical mass and viable synthesis are reached, at which point they surface and become a story. I have been a fan of J. G. Ballard's Vermilion Sands stories for years and when I projected the idea of living gems into a setting with Ballard's mood, "The Siren Garden" emerged.

Jakobsson did not like *that* story, either, as it happened, but Ed Ferman at *Fantasy and Science Fiction* did, and the Aventine stories began appearing.

For a long time, an image haunted me—that of red footprints across a stretch of white sand—until it finally gave me "Bête et Noir." "Shadow Dance" and "Broken Stairways, Walls of Time" grew out of titles, the former heard first as a song title and the latter, part of a line of poetry. Fascination with the dissociated personality as portrayed in *The Three Faces of Eve* and *Sybil* led to "A House Divided," while speculations on the standards of beauty evolved into "Ménage Outré." That most of the stories involve the arts appears to be the choice of my subconscious, encouraged by my interest in art, static and performed, or perhaps it is a recognition that art portrays many worlds of varying reality, as Aventine is a place of varying reality, and that it supports and is supported by dreams.

So come to colorful Aventine, city of sun and shadow. Leave Everyday. Share the dreams of its residents—and the nightmares.

AVENTINE

The Siren Garden

iooooooooooooooooooooo

SILICIVITAE gardens are all the fashion these days. Since some enterprising innkeeper bought Dalria, renamed it the Siren Garden, and made it the place to see and be seen in Gateside, not a week passes without some wealthy woman sitting down in my office with an open checkbook and inquiring how much I charge for crystalscaping. I leave Lee Emrys, my partner, to find a diplomatic way of refusing her. I laid out the garden at Dalria, but I did it for love, for Lorna Dalriadian, and I will never do another. I refuse to even visit Dalria again. Lee sees to whatever maintenance is necessary.

I dream of it, though. I walk down the winding stairs and paths, past the softly singing clusters, and sit down to rest on a shaded stone bench. I am listening to the counterpoint of bells and vibratos when I hear a laugh that carries even above the musical chords. I look up to see Lorna Dalriadian coming toward me, her eyes in shadow beneath her long, pale bangs. I reach out to brush the hair aside, but there is a crash and then a terrible scream rising higher and higher until I wake up. On such nights, I do not sleep again but sit awake until dawn, shivering with something that is both grief and rage.

It was late spring when she walked into my reception room the first time, one of those brilliantly clear mountain afternoons that brings Gateside's bright buildings aglow with luminous color. She walked in, looked up at me, and struck me mute and stumble-footed. It was not her beauty. Women of her class are

1

always beautiful, through the surgeon's art, if not nature's, and we have enough subscribers among them that their mere presence inspires no awe. She could have been a hag with the same effect. All I saw of her was her eyes, the largest, most intense eyes that ever mirrored a soul. They were rainbows, kaleidoscopes, the aurora borealis.

The pulsating color hypnotized me. I could have stood indefinitely watching them change from rainbow to green to violet. Not until she lowered her lashes, thick and dark as feather fans, did I realize she was speaking.

She introduced herself and asked about my crystals in a light, breathy voice that inspired a momentary vision of a schoolgirl dipping in a shy curtsy.

Somewhere I found the release on my vocal cords. "Yes, we have a very good variety. Do you prefer to buy or subscribe?"

Timon's Silicivitae is a small nursery. Our greatest volume of business is from buyers, tourists who have come to see the Diana Mountain stargate and want to take home something that came through it from the stars, something alien. They buy a pendant to wear a few weeks, and when it stops singing, carefully put it away in a box to keep until it crumbles or is thrown away, the memory of the song and beauty having faded as the crystal did.

A subscription, on the other hand, is continuous. The nursery provides replacements any time the client becomes dissatisfied with the tone or color or the bloom of the crystal passes.

When I explained the choices to Lorna Dalriadian, she laughed in delight. "I know they're alive, but do you mean they fade like flowers?"

"Similarly." I led her over to the demonstration table and dropped a cassette of sample tones in the recorder. "Are you interested in a constant, variable, or intermittent tone?"

She shrugged, her eyes changing from silver to the blue of a tropical lagoon. "Let me hear them all."

I switched on the tape and played a run of tinkler and chime intermittents, then a vibrato variable, and finally some bell constants. "There are lower-toned varieties as well, but young women like yourself generally find them too staid."

"My husband would approve of them, then." Her voice carried a wry note. "Peter says I should project a more adult image."

I knew Peter Dalriadian by reputation, a man considerably older than Lorna. They called him "The Kingmaker." He was the friend to have when seeking political office, a puller of strings. I wondered how he had found his way out of the smoke-filled rooms long enough to meet this creature of sunshine and dawn.

"I can't decide," she said helplessly. She turned to me in appeal. "You have more experience with these. Will you choose something for me?"

"If you wish, Mrs. Dalriadian."

"Call me Lorna, please." Her nose wrinkled. "Mrs. Dalriadian makes me think of Peter's first wife."

I was never happier to oblige a client. "Lorna, then."

She smiled.

I had trouble talking again. What that smile did to her eyes was more than a mortal man could withstand. "I think," I said in a voice as breathless as hers, "that a chime would suit you best, at a tone near the middle of the aural spectrum, say F above middle C. What is your favorite color?"

"Blue."

I touched the intercom. "Lee, I need a blue F plus chime with a pendant bubble and habitat."

While we waited for him, I explained the cost of the subscription and the care of the crystal. As an alien life form, the crystals cannot tolerate our environment for more than a very short time. They have to be worn in a bubble that insulates them against the temperature and atmosphere and otherwise kept in a habitat in a nutrient solution.

The disadvantage of living jewels is that they eventually die. The habitat prolongs their life only to a point. I told Lorna that Lee or I would be out biweekly to service the habitat, and we could inform her when it was time to exchange the crystal for a fresh one.

She was paying me when Lee came in with the habitat under one arm and an insulated carton in the other hand. From the carton came a soft musical note.

Lorna looked up, eyes golden. "Let me see."

Lee opened the box. Enclosed in its pendant bubble, the Siren was nestled in ice, a near-dodecahedral crystal of vibrant cobalt blue. It sounded while she looked down on it. The clear note lingered for a brief, shimmering moment in the air about us before fading. In a few seconds, the chime rang again.

"It's lovely," she breathed.

Lee closed the carton and handed it to her with a flourish, announcing he would put the habitat in her runabout.

She stood and lifted her eyes. "Good-bye. Thank you so much."

I came back to reality to find Lee lounging in the doorway with one brow hoisted to his hairline.

"That has to be the most beautiful woman in Gateside," I told him.

"An extraordinary one at any rate," he agreed.

Contrary to popular belief, Lee appreciates a beautiful woman as much as the next man. He just happens to think of them more as fine works of art rather than people and tends to regard my fervent interest in them with the same tolerant amusement he might, say, a passion for nude midnight strolls down Stargate Avenue. However, his objectivity has allowed him to develop a shrewd insight and understanding denied most men.

"Don't let this new infatuation interfere with your attention to our other subscribers," he cautioned, smiling.

He also reads me with uncomfortable accuracy.

I repeated Lee's warning to myself many times, but her eyes haunted me. I dreamed of them at night and felt engulfed in them during the day among the glittering crystals in the vivarium. I even considered taking over Lee's servicing duties when it came time to check her habitat.

I think I lived in a half daze until one day a week after our first encounter when the red flash of the call light warned me someone had entered the reception room. Between the soundproofing of the vivarium and that in our life-suit helmets, we can hear nothing. So there is the light. The inconvenience is a necessity. The much-vaunted singing of Sirens is tolerable only in selective moderation. The cacophony produced by a full-spectrum population of crystals can rupture a man's eardrums. Seven members of the Outreach Five expedition to Wynter's Planet had returned permanently deaf.

I left Lee to supervise the grazing of the vibrato beds and went up front to see the client.

It was Lorna. Eyes clouded, she held out a plastic carton. "It's dead," she said with the solemn hurt of a child.

I opened the carton. The Siren was scarcely recognizable. It lay silent, its color turned to ash gray, the edges of the facets cracked and crumbling. Dead crystals are fragile things, particularly ones that have burned up in exposure to our atmosphere.

"What happened?" I asked.

"I was showing it to a friend and had to leave the room. My friend took it out of the habitat for a closer look. When the sound changed, she dropped it and was afraid to touch it again. By the time I came back, it was like this." Her eyes were all smoke and green coals. "It screamed," she whispered. "It was a terrible sound, like something in mortal agony."

I knew the sound. No human death shriek could match the horror of it.

"Do they feel pain?" she asked.

"No one knows. It could be a mechanical effect, the temperature change shortening the chime interval and raising the frequency so that it sounds like a scream, but we can't say for certain."

"It sounded like pain. I heard it even at the other end of the house."

"Is your friend all right?" I asked. "The ultrahigh frequencies the crystals produce at times like that can have serious effects."

She looked at me intently for a moment, then past me, her expression thoughtful. She said remotely, "It gave her a headache, and a mirror broke." Her eyes focused again and looked down at the thing in the carton. "What will you do with it?"

"On the chance that there's still some usable genetic material, I'll feed it to a grazer."

She blinked.

"A grazer is a class of silicivitae which feeds on the Siren varieties," I explained.

Her eyes went wide and laughter-silver. "A rock that eats other rocks? Show me."

"Timon exists to serve his clients." Taking her elbow, I guided her to an observation panel overlooking the vivarium.

I let her stand undisturbed for a few minutes to absorb the sight of table after table of crystals of every color spread beneath the glaring white light of the sun panels. The polarization of the observation panel screened only the harmful wavelengths; it did nothing to diminish the glitter. Lee was moving between the tables, turned to an alien creature by his helmeted life suit.

Lorna sighed and reached out to press her hands against the panel, as though trying to reach the crystals.

"Lee is carrying a grazer now," I said.

He placed a reddish blob on one of the beds. Freed, it sat motionless for a short time, then slowly began to ooze across the bed toward the crystals, looking like nothing so much as an overgrown amoeba. I explained how the reproductive process of the Sirens utilizes the digestive system of the larger silicivitae to mingle their raw genetic material and form spores that are deposited with the grazers' waste material.

She stared in across the vivarium. "Then that's why they sing," she said wonderingly. "To attract the grazers."

Her perceptiveness startled me. To my knowledge, none of my other clients had ever thought to wonder why the crystals produce their varying sounds, let alone been able to deduce the reason. There appeared to be a fine mind behind those magnificent eyes.

"It's marvelous," she said. "I suppose bigger rocks eat the grazers and bigger rocks eat *them.*"

"On Wynter's Planet, yes."

She leaned against the panel. The aurora borealis of her eyes shone irridescent. "It must be exciting working with such fascinating creatures."

I nodded.

She sighed heavily. "My life is stiflingly commonplace." A short silence followed while her eyes wandered over the tables. "Would you let me go in and pick out a new Siren myself?"

I regretted refusing her, but it would have been a great deal of trouble with little point. She could not have heard through the helmet, and I did not want the responsibility of safeguarding a novice in an alien environment.

Her eyes grayed with disappointment.

"But we do have a number of crystals freshly picked for centerpieces. You can choose from among them, Lorna."

The crystals sat in rows on shelves inside a refrigerated cabinet, their root webs immersed in pans of nutrient solution. Cold and a wave of discordant sound rolled out over us as I opened the first door. The intermittents inside clanged together and broke into an irregular arpeggio, followed by a series of chords, some harmonious, most jangling.

After deliberation, Lorna chose a wine-red tinkler.

"Centerpieces . . ." she said as I packed the crystal. "For Kathryn George's banquet tomorrow night?"

I nodded.

"I've always loved her decorations. If you're putting them together today, may I watch?"

Nothing male could have refused that violet gaze. I brought her a thermal jacket and oxygen mask—the workroom is low in oxygen and maintained below freezing for the comfort of the crystals—and wondered blissfully how I was going to concentrate with her watching me and the warm, spicy smell of her filling my nostrils.

She solved part of the problem herself. "I don't want to just stand here. Is there something I can be doing?"

I let her carry the pans of crystals from the cabinet to the work table and hand me the velvet-covered stepped blocks we used for bases. Soon I was explaining the technique of crystal arranging. A single piece was simple enough, only a matter of combining low-toned constants, variables, or intermittents with complimentary high-frequency ones. The challenge of a commission like this was making all the arrangements blend with each other as well as within themselves. I showed Lorna how to break off the root webs, leaving enough for attachment to the base in a pleasing color pattern, then how to seal the bell covers over the finished arrangements. By the time Lee arrived, his vivarium chores completed, the centerpieces were proceeding smoothly, and above her mask, Lorna's eyes reflected the colors of the crystals around her a hundredfold.

Lee lifted his brows. "I appear to be superfluous."

The call light flashed.

I sighed behind my mask. "Not just yet; I'm being paged."

The customers were six middle-aged ladies. From their conversation, I had no trouble deducing they were on their way back from visiting the stargate and happened to notice my sign. They wanted inexpensive Sirens for souvenirs.

I steered them into buying pastel tinklers and after giving them instructions for prolonging the bloom of the crystals—which they no doubt heard and would follow as poorly as every other tourist—ushered the chattering flock to the door and hurried back to the workroom.

The six ladies were only the first of many interruptions, though. In addition to a stream of tourists, there were calls from subscribers who wanted exchanges and one commissioning a small arrangement to send to his wife in the maternity ward of the hospital. Despite them, the work progressed so swiftly that by closing time we had all but six of the twenty-five centerpieces finished.

Lorna stood looking around at them, listening to the rise and fall of musical notes. "How beautiful." She smiled at me. "It's like a concert."

I grinned back. "And for my next selection, I shall play the *Wynter Garden Concerto*."

Lorna's eyes blurred. They looked through me, as remote as Andromeda.

"Lorna?" I asked anxiously.

"A garden," she said slowly. "A garden—" The aurora burned again. Her voice lilted. "Wouldn't that be beautiful!"

Lee frowned. "Not a garden of Sirens."

I explained. "They have a peculiar characteristic. Singly, they're unaffected by events around them, but the larger the number grouped together, the more sensitive they become. When people near them are highly emotional, the Sirens react, usually by raising their frequencies. The result is a sound that would shame a banshee and, if the group is large enough, shatter every glass in the vicinity. A garden could wreak havoc with the entire neighborhood."

"Really?" For an instant, her eyes flared like an animal's reflecting firelight; then, smiling, she took my hand. "This has been one of the most uncommon days of my life. May I come again sometime?"

I resisted the desire to pull her arms around my neck. "Anytime."

"I'll be sure to let you know how the centerpieces looked at the banquet. Good-bye, Lee."

He nodded.

Both our gazes followed her out.

"God, what a woman," I sighed. "Those eyes!"

" 'Eyes have all the seeming . . .' " Lee murmured.

"What?"

He turned to regard me with concern. "Be careful. Don't fall in love with her."

I snorted. "That would be foolish. You know women like her; they're faddish. They throw themselves into anything new to escape their boredom. I don't expect her to hang around here long before finding a new enthusiasm."

"And if she stays a while?"

"Just remind me how notoriously bad-tempered her husband is."

I almost convinced him.

I almost had myself convinced myself until I saw Lorna again. She came in the day after the George banquet, her mood indescribable, manic yet tragic, as though wanting to laugh but too near tears. Something wild paced behind her eyes, spilling out an incandescence that left me groping for air and earth.

"It was a disaster," she said. "Oh, not the arrangements. Those looked beautiful. I wanted to tell everyone I'd helped make them, only"—she sighed—"Peter said it would be like admitting I scrubbed floors for a hobby.

"The trouble was the seating arrangements. Kathryn put the composers Denny Keys and Lincoln Howarth across the same table from each other. Keys is a rabid traditionalist, you know. He made some disparaging remark about the harmonics of the centerpiece. Howarth took it as a direct attack on the sonics he uses, and the fight was on. They started yelling, and the crystals began whining. That set off every other arrangement in the room."

I groaned.

"It was chaos! The noise felt like—like nails being driven into my brain. I wanted to fight myself or break something. So did everyone else. They screamed at each other, and glasses and plates shattered right and left. All the windows broke. Keys and Howarth almost killed each other before they could be pulled apart."

"Cancel Mrs. George's subscription," Lee said.

Lorna patted his hand. "You still have me."

She became a regular visitor. We could expect her at least three or four times a week. I asked her how she had so much time.

"Peter is gone most of the time on political maneuvers," she replied. "He never takes me, he says, because I'm not sophisticated enough. That means he thinks I'm childish."

I never considered her childish, though it was true she asked questions like a child, by the hundreds. Some were foolish, some delightfully innocent. Many I found shrewdly intelligent.

She learned to help with the customers and carry out small chores in the vivarium. Surprisingly, she had a natural talent for design that was better than mine. With training, she might have equaled Lee. Before long, I was living almost solely for the hours she was there.

Only Lee seemed dissatisfied with the situation. He treated her with unfailing courtesy, even gallantry, but his reserve never thawed in her presence, and if he smiled, the warmth never reached his eyes.

"What do you have against her?" I demanded finally.

He looked up from the arrangement he was doing for the Guilford wedding reception. "You haven't been able to give an entire thought to the nursery since she's been around."

I grinned foolishly. "Guilty. Still, there has to be more to it than that. I'm periodically distracted by one woman or another."

He switched the positions of two tinklers with great deliberation. "This one is out of your class, Michael."

That stung. "You think I'm fortune hunting?" I asked sharply.

He did not look up. "I wonder what *she's* hunting. She's the kind of woman who can have any man she wants."

"And I suppose it's impossible she might want me?"

The tinklers jangled out of key.

Lee ran a finger across them as though to soothe them. "What can you give her that a hundred wealthier, cleverer men cannot?"

Despite his mild tone, the truth of that burned. I heard an angrily defensive note in my voice as I replied but made no effort to modify it. "She's a lonely woman. Her husband spends all his time playing power-behind-the-throne, and when he's home, he does nothing but find fault with her. Lonely people fall in love with people who love them in return."

"She isn't in love." He looked up, tone earnest. "Look at her objectively. I won't say her naiveté is necessarily a pose, but it's only her surface. Once in a while, you can see something very different in her eyes, something dark and arcane. If she wants you, it's for a reason, not for yourself."

The rising whine of the crystals rasped the edges of my nerves. I clenched my teeth irritably. "Since a 'man' of your sexual persuasion is incapable of understanding love between a man and woman, I suggest you refrain from trying to advise me on the subject."

He took a deep breath. "I don't want to see you hurt."

"Well, I don't want your solicitude! Stay out of my personal life!"

His eyes shuttered. "Please lower your voice. I'll never finish the arrangement while the crystals are screaming like this."

Typical, I thought. *Frustrate him and he sulks.*

It made the time with Lorna more pleasant than ever. When she did arrangements she laughed or sang along with the crystals. Live groupings planted in sand with the roots intact for maximum longevity were her favorite arrangements. They held an endless fascination for her.

"They're like miniature gardens," she would remark. "Is a genuine garden really impossible?"

"You're certainly set on a garden, aren't you? Yes, I'm afraid it's impossible. Remember Mrs. George's banquet?" I asked. "Imagine that effect multiplied many times."

She sighed. "But it could be so beautiful." She dug a hole in the sand with her forefinger. Pressing a hummer into the depression, she pushed the soil back over the lacy web of roots. "There must be some way to control the intensity of their reactions. You use an unbalanced nutrient to produce minor chords for funeral arrangements. Can't something of the same order be done to reduce sensitivity?"

I considered the possibility. "It might." The longer I thought about it, the harder I thought about it. If I could desensitize the crystals, there would never have to be a repeat of the George disaster. "Damn, I wish I had the time to experiment."

Lorna's eyes glittered obsidian-dark. "I have nothing *but* time."

I let her have one section of the cabinet. She filled it with crystals set in bowls of nutrient-rich sand. Curiosity compelled me to open the cabinet every few days. Each time, the sounds seemed stranger. Lorna's expression varied between abstracted and frustrated on cycles of four to five days. I decided it was wiser to let her tell me in her own time rather than ask about her progress.

Then, some weeks later, I was shocked out of my concentration over book work by a howling that raised goose pimples clear from my bones. The sound seemed to be coming from the workroom. I raced toward the source, speculating wildly. Had the cooling coils gone out?

Lorna staggered out, clawing off her oxygen mask. Gasping, she threw herself at me and buried her face against my chest. It seemed only natural to put my arms around her in return.

"Lorna, are you hurt? What happened?" I asked.

Suddenly, she threw back her head and laughed. "They just sat there. The others went wild when I screamed at them, but the blues *just sat there.*"

The sound faded, resolving into the recognizable tones of intermittents and variables. Through the open doorway, I saw the work table loaded with bowls of crystals. At one end, slightly separated from the others, sat two blues.

"You managed to desensitize them?" I said incredulously.

"Some. They mumbled a little. A garden would probably be noisy enough to irritate but certainly not harmful," she replied. The aurora of her eyes blazed in triumph.

I held her off admiringly. "What did it?"

"Magnesium deprivation." She raised onto her toes and kissed me. "When can you start my garden?"

We began the next day with copious sketches and photographs of Dalria's grounds from every angle. Then, while the landscapers prepared the beds to my specifications and the electronics people installed the domes and life-supports, I designed the arrangements.

Because we were too busy for Lee to manage the nursery business by himself, I plotted the garden only at night. The workroom was the only lighted area in the building then. Even the sun panels in the vivarium were dark. Without light, the crystals became inactive, and I found it strange to peer into the vivarium and hear only the low hum of the cooling units or to bring a crystal out of the workroom cabinet and have its tone drag, blurrily flat, for several minutes before a true note sounded, as though it resented being awakened.

Each night, I conjured Lorna Dalriadian's image out of the quiet solitude and darkness. With her before me, where I could study every detail—her voice, laughter, movements, eyes—I laid down my patterns of color and sound. Nothing strident was allowed, nothing heavy or staid, only bright, pure colors and light, dancing sound. I wanted the softest of backgrounds with melodies of tinklers, high chimes, soft bells, and whispering vibratos.

As each bed was completed, the types and positions of the final choices diagramed on full-scale drawings of the beds, I showed the chart to Lorna. After the first time, she declined to see more, claiming she could not imagine the sound from a drawing.

"I'll just wait until everything is finished."

I would have liked Lee's opinion just for reassurance, but he voiced neither interest nor curiosity, and I was too stubborn to ask after my outburst at him.

Then, the morning after finishing the last sections, I overslept. When I arrived at the nursery, Lee told me Lorna had called to say she would not be in. "Her husband has business out of the city, and this time she's gone with him."

I stared at him, outraged. Gone out of the city? As I was ready to start planting? How could she?

Lee stared back. "She *is* married to him," he said as though reading my mind. "She sounded very happy, like a bride."

I would not believe it. Peter Dalriadian never gave her a happy moment in his life. Lee was just being vindictive.

He continued. "She said to tell you, though, that she's looking forward to seeing the garden when she comes back." He paused. "I've been looking over the diagrams."

It was then that I saw the pile of charts on the desk. "What do you think?" I asked hesitantly.

"It's a portrait of Lorna, isn't it?"

I looked at him in surprise. "How did you guess?"

He lifted a brow. "It's too graphic not to recognize, far better than I think you realize. Sirens may be the only medium suited to expressing her. When do you want to begin planting?"

We spent the next several days on service rounds, notifying subscribers we would be temporarily unavailable for new commissions; then we closed the front of the nursery and devoted ourselves completely to the garden.

It was a tedious job. Each crystal, insulated in a bubble, was numbered. It had to be matched against the diagrams for bed and position, then transferred to the bed through the access hatch in the rear of the dome, removed from the bubble, and planted using waldos. The hatches were small to lessen the loss of atmosphere and cold while open. Since each bed involved dozens of crystals plus accent pieces of driftwood and obsidian and sandstone boulders, the planting could occupy the majority of a day. On our best days, we were able to finish no more than two beds each. One particularly long, narrow bed that had four separate hatches took two and a half days to plant.

But while the work was slow, we felt better instead of more tired as it progressed. Around us, the silence of the first day disappeared, replaced by music that grew louder and more varied each day. Pieces of slender, airy sculpture, most of them sonatropic, arrived to fill the vacant pedestals and fountain centers. They undulated or gently shivered in response to the sound around them. I was delighted at how closely Lorna's preferences complimented my arrangements. Benches were placed along the paths and at the landing areas of stairs. We watched the garden transform from numbers on paper to glittering reality.

I found it hard to believe it was my work. It was and yet was not what I had diagramed in the workroom. The sounds seemed so different, so much better than I had anticipated, in the open.

"It's good," I said incredulously, standing with Lee on an upper path and looking down the mountainside over the terraces.

He grinned.

"Tomorrow we'll finish the last beds," I said. "In another week—"

I turned to look up at the house and accidentally bumped a sculpture pedestal. The graceful form on top tilted. I barely managed to catch it and set it upright before it toppled.

"In another week Lorna will be home," I finished.

I arranged to be there when she took her first walk in the garden. She said only a quiet hello as she joined me near the house, but the light in her eyes shamed the sun, and her fingers closed warmly around my hand.

We followed the winding paths, climbed the curving flights of steps, paused at the fountains and statuary. As we walked, the music of the Sirens changed continuously around us. A soft, wistful collection of chords became haunting, then rippled laughingly before blending into a clear, joyous interchange. Tinklers blended with the splash of fountains, and arpeggios of chimes rang in the shade of spreading old trees. Lorna walked in silence, her fingers tightening around mine at each new wonder we encountered.

Not until we had returned to the terrace at the top of the garden did she say anything, and then it was just a whisper. "Oh, Michael." She looked up at me, and her eyes caught mine, auroras shimmering. She reached up to touch my cheek. "It's—perfect."

Her eyes looked bottomless. I let myself fall into them, fall endlessly into the kaleidoscopic color. But deep in them the color disappeared and became, unexpectedly, cold and empty, a void of darkness relieved only by a sullen red glow. In panic, I groped for a hook back to reality.

"I almost broke one of the sculptures," I said. My voice sounded tight. "You ought to have them bolted down."

"Of course, Michael." She laid her head against my chest. "I dreamed what it would be like. Every day we were away, I imagined how it would look and sound, but I never thought it could be anything like this."

I put my arms around her. "I was inspired."

She laughed. The sound struck fire deep in my chest. Her arms slid around my back, and as they did, the heat diffused until even my fingers and toes burned.

"Shall we have a showing, Michael? I'll invite every art critic in the country."

"That isn't necessary."

She looked up at me. "Don't you want the world to know what a genius you are?"

"Not particularly. I designed this for you because I—" I broke off, appalled at myself. Who was I to declare love to her. And yet why not? Who was more capable of making her happy? "Lorna," I said before I lost my nerve again, "I love you."

I never had time to analyze the sudden flare in her eyes because suddenly a male voice called, "Lorna!"

I jumped backward as though she had become electrified.

"What are you doing?"

We looked around at the man in the French doors. I knew him instantly from his pictures—always dimly in the background behind political figures.

"Hello, Peter," Lorna said.

I switched my gaze to her in surprise. I had never heard her use that coolly assured tone before.

"This is Michael Timon. He was just showing me the garden."

"Timon?" Dalriadian came forward, eyeing me with displeasure. *"This* is the one you're always chattering about? I thought Timon was that swish who works on the habitat."

"Where could you have gotten that idea, Peter?" she asked.

"From you, obviously," he snapped. "You know I wouldn't have let you spend week after week down there if I'd known Timon was a real man. You deliberately lied to me. Why?"

"Mr. Dalriadian, there's nothing—" I began.

"I'll get to you, too, but right now I'm asking my wife!"

She regarded him calmly. "I've done nothing wrong. Everyone can testify I've been completely faithful."

"Testify?" He pounced on the word. "Have you been planning for a hearing?"

"Mr. Dalriadian," I began again.

This time it was Lorna who stopped me. Laying a hand on my arm, she said, "You'd better go. I'll straighten this out."

"He's going nowhere until I say so," Dalriadian snarled.

Her voice rose for the first time. "Peter, you're making a fool of yourself."

"Unless you've done it to me first."

She had edged sideways until she was on the far side of him. To look at her, he had to turn his back on me. Down at her side, her hand made sharp gestures toward the gate. When I did not move immediately, the motion became more insistent. With reluctance, I backed away, and then only because it seemed obvious she was used to dealing with such scenes.

The sound of their voices followed me to the truck. As I climbed in, I heard the quality of the tones change. They seemed to be moving toward the garden. A low whine plucked at my neck hair, confirming my guess. The argument was in the vicinity of enough Sirens to disturb them.

I started the truck, feeling relieved. The noise of the crystals would stop the quarrel before long.

Lyrae Drive serpentined around the mountainside. At one point, it doubled back on itself and opened onto a vista terrace almost directly above Dalria. Driving past, I could look over the edge and see most of the grounds. I slowed the truck to a stop to watch the Dalriadians.

They were still fighting. Lorna stood in the middle of a path, chin high. I could not see her expression from my distance, but her stance looked defiant. Her husband stood threateningly over her. He grabbed her by the shoulders. She shook her head, emphatically protesting something. He started shaking her.

Suddenly, Lorna twisted loose and fled up the nearest steps toward the house.

Her husband followed for one flight. She was too young and fast for him to catch, however. He stopped, leaning against a sculpture pedestal, and shook his fist after her.

She kept running.

As Lorna disappeared into the house, he stared after her, then turned his head to look at the domed crystal groupings around him. He put his hands over his ears. I could well imagine the effect the sound even desensitized Sirens produced must be having on his nerves. Clenching his fists, Dalriadian took a step toward the nearest bed. He stopped, then without warning, spun and picked up the sculpture in both hands.

"No!" I knew I was too far away for him to hear, but I shouted, anyway. "Don't!"

He swung the sculpture like an ax and smashed at the top of the dome. The dome had been built to withstand objects falling on it but not deliberate assault. It shattered raggedly. Still gripping the sculpture, he turned toward a second bed.

I clutched at the wheel of the truck, steeling myself for what I was powerless to prevent.

It happened even before he made the first blow on the dome. He stiffened. Dropping the sculpture, he clutched at his head. I was too far away to hear him scream, but I imagined it, and it blended with the faint, distant death shriek of the burning Sirens. Dalriadian ran in a circle clawing at his head, then staggered and fell. He twitched. Moments later, he lay still. Only the sculpture moved, writhing on the ground beside him, its tropism responding to the last fading screams of the Sirens.

I slammed the truck into gear and spun it in a tight turn back toward Dalria.

He was dead, of course. I felt sure of it even before I touched him. The one bed of silicivitae was dead, too. The others sang softly once more, their irritation forgotten now that the source had gone. I dropped Peter Dalriadian's wrist and climbed up to the house.

As I reached the terrace, movement in an upper window caught my eye. I looked up. Lorna peered out between the drapes. I reached upward involuntarily as though that could keep her back. I could see her husband's body from where I stood, so she, higher still, would, too.

She did. Seemingly unaware of me, she looked down into the garden. I bit my lip in sympathy with the anguish that would fill her face any moment.

But anguish never appeared. Instead, she smiled.

Something cold crawled up from my toes to my belly and wrapped a sharp-nailed hand around my heart.

The drape dropped back into place once more.

I stared upward. I would not believe what that smile suggested; yet how perfectly everything fitted: her interest in Sirens after the accident and her friend's headache, her abstraction when I mentioned the potential deadliness of Siren groupings, her determination to have a garden, the sculptures left loose on their pedestals. Then there was that scene on the terrace where her violent-tempered, hypercritical husband would see it. Very clever. What prosecutor in the world would think of trying to prove Lorna helped Peter Dalriadian murder himself?

How much, then, had been a lie? Had she ever felt anything but the desire for the swift completion of her plans?

I wanted to go to her, to plead for reassurance and

fall into the golden eternity of her eyes. Torn, I looked up at the window.

Sirens sang in the garden. Hearing them, I remembered that her eyes were not golden but dark and empty. Using every shred of self-will, I wrenched myself away, digging my fingers in my ears, and ran for the truck.

Tropic of Eden

EDEN LYLE still lives in Aventine. I see her occasionally at a distance, slim and graceful as ever in the Neo-hellan dresses that were her trademark, but her face is always veiled. I sometimes wonder what she thinks, living there above the Lunamere, looking out over a world she no longer allows to see her, and what she has to say to Hebe—and how much she hates me.

The news she had taken Mad Simon's villa shook Aventine like an earthquake, a rare event. Normally, the rich and famous are considered commonplace. With the international jetport and the stargate on Diana Mountain just an hour away by cabletrain, we are virtually next door to anywhere in the galaxy, yet remote enough to make a good retreat. Jessica Vanier wrote her poetry in a cabin on Birch Cove, Xhosar Kain cast his sonic masterpiece *I, the Living* in the studio next to mine, and Thomas Bradley Jerome lived on the cliffs above the Heliomere long before Congress investigated him in its hearings on black-market transplants. But Eden Lyle was another matter. She was not merely an actress, not only one of the most beautiful women alive; she was a legend, Eve and Lillith, Penelope and Circe. She had been the personal guest of every major world leader over the past decade and slept, so gossip claimed, with over half of them.

"And she arrived here last night," Clive Harrison announced dramatically, bringing the news to me at my studio. He opened his arms to the sculpture I was

22

working on. " 'Hail, moonflower, who pales the sun /
My poor heart sickens for love of you / And lives its
days as night eternal / All while—"

"For gods sake, Clive," I interrupted, "you should
know better than to talk at a sculpture with a
sonatropism. Look what the sounds are doing to it!"

The sculpture twisted like a corkscrew, leaning toward him.

Clive grinned sheepishly. "Maybe you could let me
finish and then title it *The Lovesick Poet*." But he
patted the trope and backed away.

I started humming, coaxing the trope out of its
spiral. Sound would always affect it to some degree,
of course; the dynamic nature of the medium is the
beauty of tropic sculpture. Once I had my basic concept imprinted, the piece would be permeated with a
stabilizing gas, and its subsequent alterations would be
only variations on the theme, but now every sound
affected it profoundly.

Just as I almost had the piece back to its original
form, I heard the door behind me open. I grimaced.
What I did not need now was another interruption.
Throwing a muffling cloth over the trope, I turned,
frowning.

With the light of the summer sun behind her, I
could not really see the woman in the doorway, only
her silhouette, sheathed from head to wrists and ankles in a cowled Neo-hellan dress. It was a very nice
silhouette, though, and something in the poised assurance of her carriage stopped the unfriendly greeting
in my throat long enough for her to speak first.

"Drummond Caspar?" she asked.

The voice, low and rich, husky almost to the point
of masculinity, was instantly identifiable. I think I
swallowed audibly before speaking.

"Miss—Lyle?"

Eden Lyle came forward, pushing back the cowl.
Around me the world blurred, and all I could see
in the universe was flawless skin, regal cheekbones,
eyes deeply purple and velvet as pansy petals, and
silver-blonde hair hanging straight and silky to her
waist. It had to be one of the few remaining naturally

beautiful faces in the world, just perceptibly asymmetrical, free of the monotonous perfection of cosmetisculpture. Seeing her in person, I could well believe the story that following a hovercraft accident some years ago, she had chosen to spend time in traction waiting for the shattered bones of her leg to heal rather than risk a transplant that might not match perfectly.

Behind me, Clive sighed. Softly, he began, " 'Hail, Moonflower.' "

It occurred to me that I should say something, not just stand staring. "May I help you?"

She smiled. It sent a hot flash clear to my toes. "I hope so," she said. "I need something to fill the sterile spots in the villa I've just taken. I'm told you have the best tropic sculpture in Aventine and Gateside."

Margo Chen, my agent, would have loved to record that. "I have what I consider some very nice pieces," I replied.

"Do you have photo- and sonatropes?"

I did. I worked with most of the available tropisms: photo-, sona-, thermo-, and kinetitropes—even a few psychotropes. With Clive following, I took her to the corner I used for a gallery; while she studied the sculptures, we studied her. Once, crossing glances, Clive and I exchanged blissful smiles.

"It's very difficult to decide; they're all so magnificent." Eden backed off until she stood in the middle of the area and turned slowly, tapping her lower lip with a thoughtful finger. "I think I'll take the one called *Sunspots,* and *Mercury's Child* over there." She sighed. "But none of the sonatropes are quite what I had in mind to fill—"

"I like that one over there."

Neither she nor Clive had spoken, and I certainly had not. Our heads snapped in the direction of the timid voice. It was something of a shock to realize there was a fourth person in the studio and a double shock a moment later when, on thinking back, I realized I had actually been aware of the girl all the time but had somehow avoided seeing her.

I looked at her now. She appeared about sixteen or

seventeen and closely resembled Eden, which was, perhaps, what made the differences all the more striking. I saw the same body, same bones, same coloring —but the silver hair had been crudely hacked short and, without makeup, her pale face looked virtually featureless. She wore her dress, a copy of Eden's, like a shapeless rag.

With all of us staring at her, her face did take on color, an unattractive bright pink. She stepped back, stumbling over a low kinetitrope that had reacted to her movement near it by stretching sideways. The girl recovered her balance by turning the fall into a smooth backward somersault but straightened pinker than ever. She pointed to a small pyramid of interlocking loops. Almost inaudibly, she repeated, "That one?"

It was an early piece, *Mobius Mountain,* a very minor work. I kept it more out of sentiment than any hope of selling it. It had been one of the first tropes I attempted, and I was still amused at the way it rattled its rings in response to being whistled or talked at.

Eden looked it over from a distance and shook her head. "I'm afraid it isn't suitable." She looked around once more. "I'm sorry; I don't see anything else that attracts me at the moment. I'll take just the phototropes." She paused. "Can I arrange to have them delivered?"

"I'll be happy to bring them 'round," I said.

She smiled. "Thank you. Do you know where I am?"

I nodded.

A credit card appeared from her purse. "Add a ten percent bonus to cover your trouble."

I began, "That isn't—"

Her hand on my arm interrupted me. "Please." Both her voice and velvet eyes insisted.

I made out the ticket.

The girl spoke, and though soft, the sound of her voice startled me again. Somehow I had forgotten her. "Could I have the little piece—for my room?"

"No," Eden said. She held out a hand to me. "Thank you so much for your time."

The hand felt soft and cool. I found myself kissing it. Though tempted to say something like "My time is ever slave to yours," I controlled the impulse. Clive was the poet, not I. Instead, I said, "I'll bring the pieces out this afternoon."

Clive and I followed her to the door and watched them climb into a chauffered limousine. As it hummed away, I heard Clive whistle.

He pointed at the license. "That's Bradley Jerome's number. What do you suppose she has to do with him?"

"I'm more curious about the girl," I said.

"Her?" Clive shrugged. "Don't you read the gossip columns? That's just Hebe, a cousin. Eden is her guardian."

Which explained the likeness. I dismissed the girl. "What do you think of Eden Lyle in person?" I asked him.

He sighed ecstatically. "I'm going to finish my moonflower poem and nail it to her door."

The world was coming back into focus. I shook the last heady clouds of enchantment from my brain and pushed him out the door. "Fine. Finish it. Meanwhile, I'd better get back to work on the sonatrope before the traffic through here ruins it."

I uncovered the trope but just sat staring at it. Imposing precise, brisk lines on it was impossible when all I could think about was velvet purple eyes and long silver hair. Finally, I gave up, rewrapped the trope, and called Margo in Gateside to tell her about the sale.

Her reaction was one hundred percent commercial. "Get her to sit for you."

My reaction to that was laughter. "Right. Offer her five an hour and please don't play compsynth tapes while I'm working."

"I mean it, Cas," Margo insisted. "Her portraits are worth money. Or think of its drawing value at exhibitions."

"I don't see how I can impose on her by asking her to give up her time for my profit, much as I'm attracted by the idea of being able to see her every day."

"Ah, another conquest." Margo's voice came back drily over the line. "What is it about the woman that makes weak men slaves and strong men swoon?"

"She's very beautiful."

"And beautiful women like to be admired, my lad, so get on out and sweet talk her into sitting for you."

Margo knows her business, and I usually follow her suggestions, but Eden Lyle—Eden was different. I thought about it, though. I was still thinking about it when I loaded the phototropes in the van and headed out Cliffside Road toward Mad Simon's.

There were several theories regarding Simon Broussard's architectural preferences: he was a claustrophobe; he was paranoid and wanted to see his enemies coming; or he needed to feel surrounded by the elements in order to write his music. Whatever the reason, he had had the cantilevered cliff villa built completely of polarized plastics, even to the roof and floor. Outside it was a coppery mirror, but inside, a transparent shell awash in dusky sunlight and splashed with rainbows reflected from the water of the Lunamere thirteen meters below.

I tried not to look down as I dollied the sculptures to the sites Eden had chosen for them. The sites were perfect. The phototropes would catch every change of light from dawn until sunset, and the size and form of each complemented its surroundings. Eden's choices could not have been better, and I told her so.

She blew me a kiss. "Only because I had quality work to choose from. Brad was right." Her gaze slid past me, as she thought. "I still need one more space filled. Perhaps you'll have a suggestion."

She led the way to an atrium in the middle of the house. At one end, water splashed down the sides of a flat-topped pyramid of stones into an oval pool, though that was not the first feature to attract my attention. The girl Hebe was there, too, working out nude on a broad exercise mat. I saw now how she had managed the morning's somersault over the kinetitrope. Her every movement was smooth and controlled. She flowed from stretch to bend to twist with the fluid grace of a cat.

She stopped as we came in and looked questioningly at Eden.

Eden circled the mat to the pool. "Don't let us interrupt you."

Wordlessly, Hebe resumed her exercises, though they now had a self-conscious stiffness.

Eden pointed to the waterfall. "That's where I wanted to put a sonatrope. I thought the water would provide an interesting stimulus for it." She looked up at me. "Could you do a piece especially to put there?"

It was too good a chance to miss. "Yes," I said, "but I'd like to use a psychotrope instead, and—I'd like it to represent you."

Her brows rose. "A psychotropic portrait." She studied the waterfall. "What an intriguing idea." When she looked back up at me, the velvet of her eyes had thickened to near black. "I'd like that. When would you like to begin?"

My answer emerged a bit hoarsely. "Whenever it's convenient for you."

"Tomorrow morning is convenient, but I have one condition. I dislike going out except when necessary. Would you mind bringing your materials and working here?"

Work there, alone with her, every day? I could hardly say *yes* fast enough.

She looked at the waterfall, smiling, absently pushing her hair back from her forehead. I noticed a thin, nearly invisible surgical scar just under the hairline. I peered more closely. It was the type made by face lifting. I could not guess her age, but I realized then that she could not be the young woman she first appeared to be.

Noticing my scrutiny, Eden abruptly backed away from me into the comparative shadow of the salon entrance. "I think there's nothing more to discuss, then," she said. "I'll see you at ten o'clock tomorrow. Hebe, finish inside, out of the sun."

It was clearly dismissal. Leaving, I cursed myself for staring. I was lucky Eden had not been so offended that she canceled the sittings.

The next morning, though, I wondered whether I

had imagined her offense. She greeted me with a smile that would have melted the polar caps. "Do come in. May I call you Drummond?"

"Everyone calls me Cas."

"Cas, then. I have a space cleared for you in the salon."

Aside from the uncomfortable feeling the transparent floor gave me of walking on air, I approved of her choice. The entire room was bright, but the light shone best over the small table she had set up for me. I suggested an area rug be laid where I would be working. That solved the problem of vertigo, and I was ready to go to work.

The dress Eden wore that day had been based on Minoan styles. It bared her breasts and was slit to the hip, revealing a long expanse of smooth leg with each step. She curled up on a couch in front of me. "I've never sat for tropic sculpture before. Do I do anything in particular?"

"Just relax and be yourself," I said. "With this tropism, both of us are needed to imprint the concept. I do the basic shaping; then your personality determines the final form. Don't be disturbed, but I'm going to just look at you for a while," I warned her.

She laughed. "I've been looked at by a good many people. I thrive on it."

She certainly appeared to. While I leaned on the wrapped block, forearms folded, and studied her through half-closed eyes, building an image in my mind, she stared back with velvet eyes and a slight smile curving her mouth. Then I unwrapped the block and began roughing out my mental image with chisel and hammer. It was to be slim and softly curved, all lightness, delicacy, and grace, yet sensual, too.

Eden watched in fascination. "It's extraordinary how they change shape. I know they're mutated from sensitive plants like the mimosa group, but I've al-always wondered how they come to artists like you in those nice big blocks."

"They're cultured from the breeder's parent stock from slips or, more commonly, by cloning."

Her eyes widened. "I didn't know cloning was done commercially."

"Of course. It's the best way to reproduce the qualities in a particular individual. There was even a fad for cloning people a while back."

"I remember." She glanced at a table chronometer and stood up. "I'm afraid that's all the time I have today." She softened the dismissal with a smile and a blown kiss. "Tomorrow at the same time?"

Of course, tomorrow at the same time. My only concern was what to do the rest of the day that would not seem anticlimactic.

On the way out, I passed Hebe standing still and silent in the doorway, but not until I reached the van did it occur to me that I had not so much as nodded a greeting to her. What was it about the girl that made her so easy to ignore? It must be difficult growing up a ward of someone as overwhelming as Eden Lyle. I resolved to make a point of acknowledging her presence the next time I saw her.

As it turned out, I need not have worried about the rest of my day. It was spent entertaining half the population of the artist's section, it seemed, a constant parade of people from Callisto Avenue asking what Eden Lyle was like. The traffic became so bad I finally locked the door and pretended to be out.

Eden reacted with amusement when I told her about it several days later. "I should have warned you what you were letting yourself in for. I'm sorry." The warm velvet of her eyes belied the words, though. "Do you want to stop?"

I did not. However much trouble it might cause the rest of the day, I would not have given away one of those mornings with Eden Lyle at any price.

I heard a soft slither on the floor behind me and looked around to find Hebe slipping barefooted into the room. I remembered my resolve. "Hello," I said.

She stopped short, eyes startled, and looked quickly past me toward Eden. "Hello," she whispered, and turning, fled.

I cocked a brow at Eden. "Did I do something wrong?"

"She's just shy." Eden came over to stroke the emerging shape of the sculpture. "It's progressing beautifully."

I wished it had been. I would not tell her, but the trope was resisting me. The form was only partially what I intended. The rest was its own idea. I lay awake some nights wondering what was wrong with it.

However, there was a bright side to the problem, too. Every difficulty meant another day I could spend with Eden, and they were hours I would remember the rest of my life. While I worked she—performed would be the best word, I suppose, which added the force of her personality to the shaping of the sculpture. She recreated bits of past roles, told witty anecdotes about the famous and powerful men she knew, and danced or sang. The sinuously graceful dance steps reminded me of Hebe's exercises. The songs I found mostly unfamiliar. One of them haunted me for days, though, until I finally identified it as one my mother used to sing when I was a boy.

I told Eden. It was the second *faux pas* of the day. The first had been bringing *Mobius Mountain* out as a gift for Hebe. I am not sure why I did it. Out of guilt, perhaps, compensation for having mostly ignored the girl day after day.

Once she passed her initial disbelief, Hebe shone radiant with delight. She hugged the little sculpture to her. "Thank you!" She even managed a normal tone of voice. "No one ever—" She broke off, coloring, and bolted.

Eden said, "You didn't have to do that." Her voice sounded light, polite, correct for the situation, but her face was taut, and before her eyes went opaque, I caught a quick flash of disapproval and something that looked strangely like fear.

Tension stretched uncomfortably between us. To break it, I said, "I know where one of your songs comes from," and told her about my mother.

The velvet in her eyes turned to gem-hard brilliance. Without a word she turned and walked out of the salon. I could only stare after her and wonder irritably what in the stars possessed the two of them.

Was there something about Mad Simon's villa that drove its occupants as crazy as the old man had been? Maybe living suspended in midair did it.

On the way out, I glimpsed Eden in the library, talking on the telephone. ". . . arrangements, Brad," she was saying. Her voice rose, sharpening. "It must be done as soon as possible."

I shut the door behind me rather harder than necessary.

A ringing phone greeted me at the studio. It was Eden, contrite and apologetic. "I'm sorry for my rudeness, Cas. I hope you'll forgive me."

"Of course." I was only too happy to. "But would you tell me what I did wrong?"

"I feel silly. It wasn't you at all, except that you suddenly reminded me of something I had to do, and I was out of the room before I realized I had left without explaining to you."

I did not examine the plausibility of that too closely; I wanted to believe her.

"So don't think I'm angry with you," she went on, "but I can't sit tomorrow. I have an appointment I must keep."

"I could come in the afternoon," I offered.

"I'll probably have to be gone all day. I'm very sorry."

I was, too. The day after seemed an eternity away. What could I do in the meantime? Well, for one thing, I needed to go to Gateside to pick up supplies. I really ought to stop by Margo's office, too, and go over the details of an exhibition I had been invited to contribute to. I called Margo to warn her I was coming and early the next morning caught the cabletrain.

Margo greeted me in Gateside with a sardonic smile. "Welcome back from paradise. How does it feel to be among mere mortals again?"

"Don't forget who it was that urged me to do this portrait," I said.

She lifted a brow, then grinned. One finger drew a mark in the air.

Our ritual thrust and parry over with, she pulled out information sent by the exhibition's promoters, and we settled down to study it. Mostly, it was a matter of deciding which pieces to send and how best to send them. That took most of the morning.

As we finished and stood to stretch, Margo said, "It's a bit early, but why don't we catch lunch now—my treat—and then you can see about getting your supplies."

"If you're paying, it's a fine idea. Where shall we go?"

We went to the usual place, the Beta Cygnus. The food is excellent, it is enough out of the way that the tourists have not discovered it yet, and perhaps most importantly, it sits right across the street from Margo's office. We took one of the sidewalk tables and ordered.

The waiter brought drinks first. Margo settled back comfortably, sipping at hers. "How is the Lyle portrait coming, anyway?"

I rubbed my nose, grimacing. "I don't know. I know what I *want* to do. Sometimes the piece flows right into the image, but other days it's like a wrestling match, and the best I can do is a draw. The trope is very stubborn about doing something else."

She leaned forward, setting her drink aside. "Like what?"

"That's what I don't know."

"It *is* a psychotrope," she pointed out. "Maybe the problem lies in your subject, or to be more exact"—she hurried on when I opened my mouth to protest—"the difference between your subject and your concept of her. The trope may be responding exactly as it should."

I rejected that flatly. Eden was nothing like the form the psychotrope appeared to be trying to take. There was one other possibility, of course. Until it was stabilized, the trope could shape to any personality near it, and Eden did not live alone. I would not have thought, however, that Hebe's personality would be strong enough to override—

The thought broke off as I saw the subject herself at a back table. Surprisingly, Hebe sat alone. I called to her.

She hesitated, then smiled and waved shyly.

"Come join us," I invited.

After a good deal of lip chewing, she did, holding her long skirt up to keep it from tangling with chair legs or her own feet. I introduced her to Margo, who looked the girl over with the same narrow-eyed speculation she used on the work of unknown artists.

"Gateside is an interesting place to poke around on your own, isn't it?" I asked.

Hebe's eyes widened with surprise. "I'm not alone. Eden is inside."

"She finished her appointment, then?"

"Appointment?" The eyes, so like Eden's but without Eden's life and humor, widened still further. "I don't know. This is where Mr. Jerome brought us. When Dr. Ascher came, Eden told me to wait out here."

It had to be the longest single speech I had ever heard her deliver.

Margo frowned. "Ascher. Dr. *Hugo* Ascher?"

Hebe bit her lip. "I don't know." Her eyes went past us toward the door of the Beta Cygnus. She brightened. "Ask him yourself. They're coming out."

Eden recognized me instantly. The brim of her hat hid her expression, but surprise showed in her posture as she halted in the doorway. She moved forward again almost immediately, and by the time she reached our table, she was smiling in delight. I stood up to meet her.

She held out both hands to me. "Isn't this a marvelous coincidence? We get to see each other today, after all, it seems. Oh, I'm forgetting my manners." She stepped aside and brought up the men behind her. "Drummond Caspar, Brad Jerome. You may have seen him around Aventine. And this is Mr. Hans Feldman."

Jerome nodded. The other man made a stiff little forward jerk that looked like an aborted bow from the waist.

Eden sighed wistfully. "I wish we had time for a drink with you, but we have to go." She reached up and touched my cheek. "Tomorrow. Hebe."

She called the girl as someone might command a dog to heel. It was a disquieting thought I wished I had not had.

Margo looked after them. "Feldman?" she murmured.

"Maybe Hebe heard wrong. She's a strange child."

"Strange, maybe, but not wrong. The man's name is Ascher all right, and he used to be a doctor until someone sued him for malpractice a few years ago— I forgot the circumstances just now—and his license was taken away."

I vaguely remembered the case, too.

Margo sipped her drink. "I wonder why she lied."

"Maybe Jerome told her to." After all, it was easy to see the possible connection between Mr. Thomas Bradley Jerome and an ex-doctor. Eden was probably along for the ride, and naturally Jerome would caution her against advertising his affairs. I put the matter out of mind.

To be more accurate, I made the decision to do so. In actual fact, it would not go away. It kept niggling at me, asking uncomfortable questions like: if Jerome wanted a confidential meeting, why not temporarily dismiss Eden, as they had Hebe?

That may have been why the sittings went so poorly after that. Psychotropes are the most difficult to manipulate; they need full concentration and no external tension. Either I lack the one, or something was providing too much of the other because I had no control over the sculpture any longer. It kept pulling away from my hands, slowly, in the way of tropes, but inexorably. The fluted edges defied being spread and insisted on curling like scrolls. I would coax one into opening, but when I turned my attention to another, the first started folding again.

"It seems to have gone psycho today," I said, trying to make a joke of it one day, giving up on it in disgust.

Eden tucked her arm through mine and rubbed her cheek against my shoulder. "Perhaps it's a faulty piece of material. Or maybe"—she looked up at me—"it's something I'm doing wrong."

"I'm sure it isn't your fault. But I really don't care any longer. I'm tired of fighting it. Why don't we scrap it? I'll get a new block and start over."

Her finger smoothed the hair on my forearm. "There isn't time. Brad is going abroad soon, and he's asked me to come with him."

The bottom went out of my stomach. "And you're going?"

"Oh, Cas." Raising herself on her toes, she kissed me. "It isn't the end of the world, nor is it forever."

It would only seem so. I looked down at her. "So you want me to keep working on this piece as it is?"

She stepped away from me and turned her attention on the trope. "I don't think it needs any more work."

I stared incredulously. "How can you say that when—"

She interrupted. "It may not be what you intended —sometimes a role I set out to play won't take the interpretation I would like, either—but it's still beautiful. I'd like to keep it as it is."

I eyed the trope with distaste. It was a piece of garbage. "I won't sign it."

"That's all right." She grinned mischievously. "I'll still know who did it."

I went on as though she had not spoken. "But I won't charge you for it, either. I don't approve, but if you want it, it's yours. I make you a gift of it."

The velvet of her eyes glowed richly. "Thank you."

I carried it out to the atrium and placed it on the flat surface above the waterfall. Then, leaving Eden admiring it, I gathered up my tools and glumly loaded them in the van. I left with only a perfunctory wave at Hebe, who was exercising on the floor of the library. I could not understand how anyone with Eden's good eye for art could think the sculpture was beautiful. It was not at all what it was supposed to be, not at all Eden Lyle.

I did not see Eden again for almost a week. I picked up the phone a couple of times to call but could think of nothing to say and hung up again. I kept hoping she would call me. She did not, and finally, afraid that if I did not act, I would lose the chance to see her at all before she left, I drove out to her villa one evening.

It was just getting dark, but the lights had not been turned on in the villa yet. It loomed opaque against the sky. A figure in a long, pale dress moved gracefully through the garden.

"Eden," I called.

The figure paused. I vaulted the low boundary wall and ran up the slight slope toward her. Not until I was beside her did I realize it was Hebe. What I had taken for long hair was the cowl of her dress.

I could not keep the disappointment out of my voice. "I thought you were—"

"I know," Hebe said. "She's out tonight."

My disappointment sharpened. The drive had been in vain. I felt I could not just leave, though, so I said, "It's uncanny how much you look like your cousin in this light. If you wore some makeup and let your hair grow, the two of you would look almost like twins."

Hebe's eyes lifted to mine—dark, unreadable pools. "We are."

I did not immediately understand. "Are what?"

"Twins. Not cousins."

I laughed. "There's just a few too many years' difference in your ages for you to be twins."

"I'm a clone," Hebe said.

I realized several moments later that my jaw was hanging and snapped it back into place. I tried to talk but did not succeed very well. "A—I thought—cousins, I was told—why would Eden—"

"I asked once," Hebe said. She sighed. "She wouldn't tell me why she had me made."

She turned toward the villa. I moved at her elbow. She pulled a leaf off a low-hanging branch and absently shredded it as we walked. I watched her covertly.

A genetic duplicate of Eden, maybe, but nothing alike in any other respect. Why did she exist? I knew the reasons usually attributed to certain groups: homosexuals, male and female, and "liberated" women in order that they might have children without having to involve the other sex; individuals whose vanity forbid the dilution of their germ plasm; eugenics faddists intent on perpetuating their ideas of racial perfection.

Surely Eden did not fall into any of those categories.

We reached the villa. Dropping the remains of the leaf, Hebe led the way inside through the terrace door. With darkness, the perception of depth was gone, and the floor looked more substantial, though the moons and stars visible beyond the ceiling and the splintered reflection of the moon on the water below still gave the illusion of being immersed in a sea of lights. Hebe touched a hidden light switch, and the illusion disappeared. Instead, mirrors surrounded us. Our distorted images reflected at us from walls, ceiling, and floor.

She shook back the cowl of her dress, watching her reflections do the same. "Hebe was a servant," she said quietly.

Her mythology was poorly researched. "Not exactly a servant," I corrected her. "Hebe was the cupbearer of the gods, yes; she was also the goddess of youth and spring. One of her gifts was supposed to be the ability to restore youth."

Hebe focused on me for a moment; then her eyes went remote. "Next to physical perfection, Eden worships youth." She turned toward the atrium. "Come look at your sculpture. It keeps changing."

I could well imagine, since it had never been stabilized. I was almost afraid to look, but, reluctantly, I did.

If it had not been mine, if I had not known how it was supposed to look, I might have been able to admire the piece. It stood tall and graceful, its color faintly luminous in the single spotlight shining up from its base, but where it should have spread wide, catching the light and embracing the horizon, it was narrow, shadowed, folded in upon itself. It stirred, reacting to our presence. Slowly, several of the fluted edges unrolled.

"Watch," Hebe said.

She moved around the pool. The sculpture quivered. It turned, following her progress.

The skin down my spine prickled. I have worked with tropes of every kind but none that ever reacted like that, not even kinetitropes. I moved around the pool in the opposite direction, but the sculpture did not react to me.

"Only me," Hebe said.

She moved closer. The trope leaned toward her, more of its edges opening, reaching, groping for her. With a shiver, Hebe backed away and walked quickly into the salon.

I followed. "When are you leaving?"

"Day after tomorrow." She did not turn on the lights but stood at the wall looking down over the Lunamere. "For Switzerland."

"Eden is partial to mountains, isn't she?"

Hebe looked around inquiringly.

"Both Aventine and Switzerland have mountains," I explained.

"We're going because of some spa Eden wants to visit." By the light coming in from the atrium, I could see her wrinkle her nose. "I even have to go."

"It won't hurt you. Most of those places provide plenty of rest, nutritious food, and exercise."

She just looked at me. After a bit, she said, "I get that here."

I laughed. "Which spa is it?"

"Nebenwasser, near Schoneweis."

Nebenwasser. I had heard of it somewhere. I groped for the memory, but it eluded me.

"Dr. Ascher recommended it," Hebe said.

I knew, then, where I had heard of Nebenwasser, and more, I remembered the details of Dr. Hugo Ascher's malpractice conviction. That answered other questions, too. I hated all of them.

"Where's Eden?" I asked hoarsely.

"With Mr. Jerome."

I did not even thank her; I just headed for the van. I had to find Eden.

I did not have to go far. She climbed out of Jerome's limousine as I left the villa. She watched it drive away before she turned and saw me.

"Why Cas," she began, "what a lovely sur—"

I grabbed her by the shoulders. "Would you really go that far to stay physically perfect?" I demanded.

Darkness hid her expression, but I heard her sharp

intake of breath. "What do you mean? Cas," she protested, "you're hurting me."

"I know what Hebe is."

"So?" Her voice cooled. "There's nothing wrong with cloning."

"But she doesn't know why you did it. I do. Eden, don't do it," I pleaded.

Her muscles went diamond hard under my hands. With a sudden, surprisingly strong movement, she twisted loose and backed away. "I don't have the slightest idea what you're babbling about," she said coldly.

Then I was sure I was right. I hardened my voice. "You've heard of Nebenwasser, surely. Your friend Jerome owns the property, according to Congress. He calls it a health spa, but it's a hospital."

"I will give you the benefit of the doubt and assume you're merely drunk, not mad. Go home and sleep it off, Mr. Caspar."

I caught her elbow and locked both hands around it. "Dr. Hugo Ascher, whom you call Feldman, is a transplant surgeon. He was one of the top men in the field until he made a bad tissue match on an experimental surgery and the patient died because the transplant rejected. There would be absolutely no chance of that if recipient and donor were genetic duplicates."

"In one second," Eden hissed, "I am going to start screaming."

I continued relentlessly. "The transplant was a brain transplant."

The scream that shredded the night around us came from behind me. I dropped Eden's arm, whirling. A pale figure fled away from us toward the villa. Hebe must have followed me out. If so—

"My god," Eden whispered. "She must have heard everything. Damn you to hell, Drummond Caspar! Hebe!" She ran after the girl. "Hebe, wait!"

The front door slammed behind them. When I reached it, it was locked. I pounded on it. Inside, Hebe screamed hysterically.

I lunged at the door, but it was massive and solid. All I did was bruise my shoulder. The screaming went on, and under it, the murmur of Eden's voice. I remembered the terrace door Hebe and I had used earlier and started around the villa toward it.

I could just make out some of Eden's words, knife edged. "Lovesick fool . . . jealousy . . . keep us here . . . he's a troublemaker . . . Nebenwasser . . . good time . . ."

"Liar," Hebe shouted. "LIAR!"

Suddenly, as I reached the terrace door, Eden shrieked, "Hebe, *no, don't!"* She screamed once, then subsided into a keening wail of despair.

From the sound of their voices, they were in the atrium. I saw their images, vague and distorted through the intervening walls. I ran for the atrium—and stood paralyzed in the doorway.

The plastic wall panels reflected the scene and reflected also the images of opposite walls, so that stretching away to infinity on all sides, with increasingly greater distortion, were countless Edens wailing beside countless pools, their arms reaching toward the waterfall at the end, where the psychotrope huddled dark and withered, and countless Hebes stood pressing their cheeks to the searing hot metal of the small spotlight they had ripped from the base of the sculpture.

I broke my paralysis and vaulted the pool to jerk the spotlight away from Hebe.

She let it go, smiling. The entire side of her face glared livid. "Too late," she said triumphantly. "I'm not perfect anymore." She swayed. "No use to her now."

I caught her as she fainted.

And around me reflections reflected reflections, and an infinity of Edens looked at me with loathing and sank to the floor of an infinity of atriums, covering their faces.

A House Divided

⦿○○○○○○○○○○○○○○○○○○○○○

AMANDA GAIL and Selene Randall came to Aventine during the autumn hiatus, when the last of the summer residents had returned to jobs in the city or followed the sun south and the winter influx of skiers and skaters was still some weeks away. Aventine scarcely noticed them, and if my current cohab had not gone off through the Diana Mountain stargate on an artists' junket, they might never have been more than clients to me, either. There are nights I cannot sleep for wishing she had chosen another realty agent or had come some other season. I was alone, though, in the boredom of autumn when Amanda walked into my office with her seeds of tragedy and elected me gardener.

"Matthew Gordon?" she asked in a soft, hesitant voice I remembered from the last election, extolling the senatorial virtues of her father. "I'm Amanda Gail. I wired you about renting a cabin?"

I nodded. "I have your wire."

Her pictures, though, did not do her justice. Not only was I surprised to find her so much taller, fully my height, but no media camera had ever captured the glow that suffused her otherwise rather plain face, giving her the look of a Renaissance madonna and adding nostalgic charm to her loose topknot of copper hair and high-waisted Regency dress.

"How many will be in your party?" I asked.

Eyes with the warm brilliance of goldstone looked at me through her lashes. "I'm alone."

I nodded again, but I wondered how Amanda Gail

could ever, really, consider herself alone. The acrimo-
nious divorce of former Olympic runner Margot Randall and Sen. Charles Gail had traumatically divided
not only Amanda's childhood but her very psyche.
Five years earlier, when Margot Randall died in a
hovercraft accident and Amanda moved to Washing-
ton full time, it emerged that for most of her childhood, Amanda Selene Gail had been two personalities,
Amanda Gail and another calling herself Selene Randall. The revelation, and their decision to remain dissociated, had made them the darlings of the gossip
columns.

"Senator Moran told me I could live here anony-
mously. Is that true?" Amanda asked.

"Absolutely. Aventine has too many rich and famous residents to care about another celebrity, and as
we have no hotels or public transportation, and the
cabletrain from Gateside is the only way in aside from
private aircraft on private landing strips, we manage
to discourage most reporters and curiosity seekers."

She smiled. "Wonderful."

That smile was wonderful, too. It turned the light in
her to dazzling incandescence.

"My runabout is outside. I'll show you what I have
available."

I carried a long list of rentals owned by summer
people who authorized winter leasing to pay for the
upkeep on their property. They were located all over
Aventine, from a few apartments down near the shopping square to cabins in the woods and along the
shores of both the Lunamere and Heliomere. I explained the choices to Amanda as I handed her into
the runabout and unplugged the car from its charger.
The Lunamere's main attraction in winter was that it
froze over, making sixteen superb kilometers of ice for
skating. Hot springs fed the Heliomere, leaving its
water a bath-water-warm thirty-five degrees, suitable
for year-round swimming.

"I'm no swimmer, but I prefer hot water to ice,"
Amanda said.

I drove her up to a little A-frame at No. 43 Apollo
on the lower shore of the Heliomere. It was a good

size for a single person, with a deck all around and steps leading down to the beach in back. Amanda admired the white expanse of the beach, which would have gratified the city council. They had spent a good deal importing all those tons of sand from some distant world on the stargate system to cover the razor-edged flint nature originally laid there.

What brought another of those incredible smiles was the interior. Not only did the carpeting continue up the walls, but as she walked from the kitchen, across the lounge area to the fireplace, and turned to look up at the sleeping loft, each place her feet touched, a patch changed color to a pale, clear yellow. She stared, then laughed and ran her hands along the back of a chair. It, too, changed color, to a pattern of pastel greens and yellows.

"Polysensitives," she said. "I haven't seen any of these since I was a little girl." She sat down in the chair. As the color change spread over the entire surface, the contours altered to a deeper, softer look. "How fun."

Unfortunately, the polys were not always fun. The terrestrial and extraterrestrial psychosensitive materials that were supposed to enable the poly furnishings to match their owner's personality and moods became so neurotic when exposed to a large number of users or to households where emotion ran hot that they developed shapes and colors whose effect on humans ranged from mildly annoying to violently nauseating. Polys were appropriate for Amanda, though. They could suit both her and her alter ego and eliminate any conflict over taste in furniture.

Amanda said, "I think this will be fine. Where do I sign the lease?"

That brought her alter to mind. "Will Selene be signing, too?"

The light in her dimmed, leaving her only a lanky girl in an anachronistic dress. She pulled at a copper lock dangling over her temple. "There's no need. The courts won't recognize us as separate people. What one does is legally binding on the other."

I was dismayed by the effect the question had on

her. I forced heartiness into my voice. "Then let's go back to the office and sign. You can move in today."

Driving down the mountain, I pointed out the villas and estates of some of our most famous citizens: actress Lillith Mannors, novelist Jason Ward, and our extraterrestrial, Gepbhal Gepbhanna. I was finally rewarded by seeing the light rekindle in her. At the office I explained that the owner of No. 43 would only let the cabin until May. Was that all right with her?

"I hope I'll be gone before then. I'm just on holiday until I decide what to do with my life."

I raised my brows. "You've given up being hostess for your father?"

She lowered her eyes. "My father remarried last month. He doesn't need me any longer. But a woman of twenty-six ought to be leaving home, anyway."

"I'm surprised there's any problem what to do. Your dancing has already won critical acclaim."

The light in her dimmed. "Selene is the dancer. I don't know anything about it."

I frowned in puzzlement. "But if *she* knows—" I began. Then, as her light went out entirely, I said hastily, "I'm sorry; I didn't mean to offend you. I was just curious . . ."

"Everyone is." Her voice carried no bitterness, but the flatness of tone served as well.

I quickly brought the subject back to business. "If you come to May and aren't ready to leave, I'll find you another place."

She tugged at the lock of hair over her temple again. "By that time, it will be Selene's decision."

My curiosity reared up again. The gossip columnists speculated a great deal about how Amanda and Selene managed their dual existence, but because neither personality gave interviews on the subject, it had to remain only speculation. The custody decision, however, was public knowledge. January to June had gone to Margot Randall, July to December to the senator. It sounded as though the alters might still divide their year that way. I wondered, but rather than distress my client further by asking, I bit my tongue and hurried out to get the lease from my secretary.

While Caro typed in the blanks, I wondered at the difference between Amanda Gail's attitude toward Selene and that portrayed by the columnists. They made it sound like kinky fun. Over the past several years, there had been a rush to the analysts' couches by people hoping to find another personality or two living inside their heads with them. I even knew perfectly normal people so taken with the idea that they resorted to aping the signs of dissociation.

Amanda still seemed very quiet when I took the lease in to her. I offered her myself and my runabout to move her luggage from the cabletrain station. She accepted, and while we collected the luggage, including a huge trunk that almost filled the car, I did my best to be kind and amusing. Finally, she began to glow again. I left her with the key, my telephone number, and a warning that since the cabins on either side of her for some distance were empty, she should keep her doors locked. I also promised to call her the next day to see if she needed anything.

"Not too early, please?" she said. "I like to sleep late."

"Why don't I come up at noon? We'll have lunch somewhere and I can show you the sights."

She hesitated, then smiled. "That sounds lovely."

I lived on the Heliomere myself, just a kilometer away from Amanda's cabin. I don't sleep late, and the next morning while I was taking my wake-up walk along the beach, I saw no reason not to pass her cabin. I could take a brief look to make sure everything was all right, then come back for her at noon as agreed. I was enjoying the frosty bite of the air in my nose and throat and the surreal effect of the steam rising off the dawn-pink Heliomere when I saw Amanda running up the beach toward me, her hair flying long and loose around her.

My initial spasm of panic passed as I realized she wore an exercise jacket and shorts and was only jogging, not running. She saw me about the same moment. She spun around as though to run away, then shrugged and waited for me to catch up.

"I thought you like to sleep late," I said.

She started walking. "Mandy does."

I almost missed the next step turning to stare at her. "You're Selene?"

She did look different. Her chin held higher added even more height to her. She met my eyes directly rather than looking through her lashes, and the color of her eyes, too, had changed, from goldstone to the feral warmth of topaz. And despite her slow walk beside me, she radiated energy so electric it fairly raised the hair on my arm nearest her. Even her voice had altered to become higher, firmer, more rapid.

"Are you in command today, then?" I asked.

"No." She shook her hair back over her shoulders. "I don't take over officially until January. I just come early each morning to exercise."

I raised my brows. "That's dedication."

"That's necessity. Without daily practice, I'll stiffen up, and my elevations will fall."

"Elevations?"

Without breaking stride, she soared into a high leap and came down grinning. "Elevations." Then she stopped and turned to face me. "I'll have to ask you for a favor. Mandy doesn't know about my practice sessions. Not being a dancer, she wouldn't understand how important this is to me. She'd just be upset knowing I was here out of my time. So when you take her to lunch today, please don't mention you saw me."

I blinked. "If you know I'm taking her to lunch, how is it she doesn't know what you're doing?"

"I'm continuously aware; she's only conscious when she's out."

That hardly seemed fair to me. As though she read my mind, Selene said, "I didn't plan it; it just works out that way."

She headed toward the cabin again, leaning forward as though straining against an invisible leash. I could almost hear the crackle of contained energy within her.

"You won't tell, will you?" she asked anxiously.

I thought about it. I could see no harm in Selene being here. "No, I won't tell her."

She sighed in relief. "Gordy, you're a friend. We'll meet again."

The leash broke. She bounded away down the sound. As though that were not release enough, she flung herself into a succession of cartwheels and forward flips. She disappeared out of sight around a curve, still cartwheeling. By the time I reached the curve, she had disappeared.

At noon, Amanda was waiting for me out on her deck. She came down the steps toward the runabout with a regal grace so unlike Selene's bridled energy it was hard to believe they possessed the same body.

"Good morning, Mr. Gordon." She smiled brilliantly. "Where are we going?"

"To a café called The Gallery."

Its main attraction, aside from its being one of the two cafés open, was that while we waited for our order, we could walk around it looking at the paintings and sculpture on exhibition by local artists.

"You must have quite an artists' colony here," Amanda said, looking over the collection. She ran a hand down the smooth curves of a sonatropic sculpture by Drummond Caspar. The trope leaned toward the sound of her voice and undulated.

"Artists founded Aventine. Between them and our celebrity citizens, shopkeepers and businessmen like me are a minority group. Aventine is really no more than a village with a large population."

"Then what are the sights you mentioned?"

"The most unique collection of architecture in the world."

Her goldstone eyes widened in disbelief. "Architecture?"

I grinned. "I, somewhat naturally, am a connoisseur of buildings, and I promise you, Miss Gail, that nowhere else will you find such a free exercise of idiosyncrasies in home design."

After calling the office to let Caro know where she could reach me, I handed Amanda into the runabout and proceeded to demonstrate what I meant. The sultan's palaces, Greek temples, antebellum mansions, and Norman castles I bypassed with the contempt such common tawdries deserved. Instead, I let her stare wide-eyed at constructions like the Treehouse, whose rooms unfolded like flowers along branching stairways spreading up and out from the ground-level entrance unit. There were the grottos and galleries of the Cavern, carved into the cliffs above the Lunamere, and the jigsaw stacked rooms of the Funhouse.

"It's marvelous," Amanda said. "And people actually live in them?"

The most marvelous part of the afternoon for me was Amanda clinging to my arm and greeting each new offering with a sigh of pleasure or gasp of delicious dismay. In the course of it, she stopped calling me Mr. Gordon, too, and began saying Matthew. I would have preferred Matt, but when I brought that up, she disagreed.

"If you don't mind," she said, looking at me through her lashes, "I prefer some formality. As my father says, this modern rush to intimacy promotes sex but prevents conversation and understanding."

I did not feel ready to dispute the great Senator Gail. "Then I take it you don't want me to call you Mandy?"

"No!" Her vehemence startled me. She quickly lowered her voice and went on, "My friends call me Amanda."

I tried to extend the day by inviting her out for dinner as I was driving her back to her cabin, but she declined with a smile. "I really should finish unpacking."

"I can help."

She shook her head. "Thank you, anyway."

I did extract a promise that she would let me show her more houses another day; then I made myself leave. I drove home reflecting what pleasant and restful company she was. A man could do far worse than she for a companion, at least until my cohab returned. I wondered, too, when I might see Selene again.

I found a note from her on my door the very next morning.

Gordy, ·

You should have insisted on dinner last night. Playing hostess for the senator never included kitchen duty. Help Mandy get a meal subscription.

It was unsigned and the writing more careful than I would have expected of Selene, but I could not imagine anyone else writing it.

I called Amanda at noon. Without mentioning the note, I asked about her cooking.

After a short pause she said, "I just throw things together."

I shuddered. "You need more than that. I'm going to call a food service in Gateside and take out a subscription for you; then I insist you eat with me, either out or at my place, until your first week's supply of meals is delivered."

I organized my arguments while I waited for her protest that she could look after herself, but to my surprise she said quietly, "You're right, of course. Thank you for taking so much trouble for me."

I considered nothing trouble that guaranteed me the chance to see her twice a day. When I met Selene on the beach several mornings later, I thanked her.

She shrugged, running in place while she talked to me. "Someone has to let you know when things need to be done."

She started off up the beach.

"May I run with you?" I called after her.

She looked back without stopping. "If you like. I enjoy having someone besides myself to talk to. It's only fair to warn you, though; I'm harder to get along with than Mandy."

She proved to be nothing if not honest. In the succeeding mornings, if I ran too slow, she simply left me behind. She said what she thought bluntly and never hesitated to disagree with me. Still, there was no verbal swordplay and no pretense about her, which I found as attractive in its way as Amanda's charming acquiescence. And I never ceased to be fascinated by the difference between Amanda's serenity and Selene's coiled-spring energy.

Selene also kept me informed on what needed to be done either around the cabin or for Amanda. Morning after morning, she handed me notes when I met her. Though always glad of an excuse to see more of Amanda, I was puzzled by the notes.

"Why write?" I asked Selene. "Why not just tell me?"

That particular morning, she was working through a set of stretching exercises that raised sympathetic screams of protest in my muscles even while I watched. She never broke the rhythm of them, and her voice came in gasps between reaches and bends. "Habit, I guess. I always left—notes for Mandy."

"Like these?"

"Basically. In the beginning—it was to tell her—about me, then—to let her know—who I had met and what—I had learned in school—my half the year—so people wouldn't know—about us."

I gave in to curiosity. "When did you become two people?"

She rolled to her feet. Swinging up onto the deck, she began using the railing as a *barre* for ballet exercises. She shot me an amused glance. "Ah, question number two. One, of course, is 'What is it like being two people?' " Then, before I could apologize, she grinned. "You, I'll tell. We split at the tender age of six. I told Mandy about it when we were seven, after we'd learned to read and write. Any more questions?"

I nodded. "What do I tell Amanda when she asks me how I always know to have something fixed? You don't want me saying anything about you, but I don't like the idea of lying to her."

Selene went on exercising. "She won't ask. People have been taking care of Mandy all her life. She takes it for granted we know what she needs." She straightened, pink and sweating with exertion. "Oh, I'd better warn you. Next week is the senator's birthday. Mandy will be asking you to take her shopping for a gift." She blew me a theatrical kiss and disappeared inside.

Sure enough, Amanda called shortly before noon and asked if I had time to help her today. Caro looked disapproving but had to admit the appointment book was empty. This time of the year, that was the normal state of business. "If something should come in, put it on for first thing tomorrow morning."

"Can I reach you anywhere in particular?"

I shook my head. "Not unless you call long distance to Gateside."

She rolled her eyes. "That's a long way for a birthday gift. Have fun."

Amanda, too, thought that at first, but I had my arguments ready. The hour's ride would be spectacular, and she would find the shopping selection immeasurably better, including warehouses of stargate imports. Also, since the train ran until midnight, we could have dinner and go to the theater before coming back. That persuaded her.

By the end of the day, I still thought it had been a good idea even though my feet ached from following her through what had to be every shop in Gateside before she found a gift she thought worthy of her father. I requested a window table at the Beta Cygnus Cafe, where we could drink some coffee and rest while we watched patrons around us and people in the street outside.

Amanda sat back sipping her coffee with a contented smile. "I hope your business isn't suffering because of all the time you've spent on me."

"I'd suffer if I couldn't spend time on you," I replied.

She smiled. "You're very gallant. Oh, look!" She pointed out the window at a passing group sporting a rainbow of fanciful hair colors and wearing leotards and tights beneath coats thrown casually around their shoulders.

"They're probably from the Blue Orion Theatre up the street. Would you like to see the show there tonight?"

"I'd love to." She looked at me through her lashes, the goldstone eyes glowing. "I can't think when I've enjoyed another man's company as much as yours."

A rising tide of babble at the door almost drowned her out. I looked around to see the group from the street pouring into the café in loud, animated conversation with each other. One of them, a tall, lithe man with hair, eye shadow, and fingernails striped fuchsia and lavender, broke off from the group to head toward us, grinning.

"Se*leene*, love," he caroled. "What a de*light*ful sur*prise!*"

Amanda recoiled. My chair scraped back as I stood up. "Who are you?"

He stopped, blinking at me. He took in Amanda's horrified expression and frowned uncertainly. "Teddy —ah—that is, Gerald Theodore. Selene and I partnered and cohabed when we were dancing in *Tall People* in London three years ago, didn't we, Selene?"

"I'm not Selene," Amanda whispered.

The dancer raised a brow. "Ah, I see. You're the other one." He grinned at me. "You know, all those months together with Selene, if I hadn't already known about her, I'd never have guessed—"

"Matthew, I'd like to leave." Amanda fumbled for her cape.

I helped her to her feet and into her cape. With a hand under her elbow, I guided her out of the Beta Cygnus, leaving the dancer staring open-mouthed after us.

I flagged a cab to take us back to the cabletrain station. Amanda said nothing for the entire ride, just stared at the clenched hands in her lap. I put an arm around her. She stiffened at my touch, then buried her face against my shoulder. At the station, waiting for the train to come in, she sat up and began pushing at her hair.

"I'm sorry. I know it seems an inconsequential thing to go to pieces about, but every time I meet one of Selene's friends, I feel like spiders are crawling over me. They're all so—grotesque." Amanda shuddered. "I don't know how she can actually live with such creatures. I suppose it's her nature. I've never let a man touch me, but she—she'll have any man that strikes her fancy, just like her mother used to."

I felt my brows hop at the vicious tone of her voice.

"My father could have been president but for Margot Randall. The woman was rapacious, vulgar, egocentric, and totally amoral. She nearly drove my father mad before he realized there was no helping her."

Her vehemence disturbed me. I disliked the criticism of Selene, too. "You don't know Selene is like that," I said in what I intended to be a soothing voice. "You've never met her."

"I've met her friends."

That obviously ended the subject as far as she was concerned. She sat quiet the remaining ride home. She reached for my hand after a few minutes, though, and held it, squeezing a bit from time to time. I was content.

At the cabin, she said, "I'm sorry for my poor company."

"That's all right. Do you feel better now?"

She gave me a faint smile. "A little. You're a good man, Matthew. If I didn't feel like Selene is leering over my shoulder, I'd kiss you good night. Another time I will. Please call me tomorrow."

I drove home wishing I could have stayed. I wondered what Selene would have to say about the incident.

Selene laughed. She spun across the sand in time to music only she could hear and grinned broadly. "Poor vestal virgin. How shocking to be confronted with the possibility that the temple of her body has been defiled."

I had expected more sympathy. "You don't sound sorry it happened," I said shortly.

She stopped with her leg in the air. She held the position a few moments, then slowly lowered the leg and brushed back a lock of hair escaping from the tight knot at the nape of her neck, all the while fixing me with a cool topaz gaze. "Why should I? Nothing happened. Teddy is a dear thing, and Mandy's archaic sensibilities are her problem, not mine."

I stared back at her. "You don't like Amanda, do you?"

She considered the accusation. "I wouldn't choose her for a friend, no. I think she's insipid and gutless. She could have sent Teddy on his way with a few polite words instead of making an incident of it. Still, I think I pity rather than dislike her. Don't I let myself get sucked into looking after her like everyone else? That saccharine, yielding dependency is only what her father trained into her. It's the senator I dislike." She snorted. "Imagine a contemporary man with a nineteenth-century taste in women. No wonder my mother left him." She resumed dancing.

I was still angry, not ready to stop the fight yet. "She left *him*? It's my understanding that her infidelities forced him to divorce her."

The jab left her untouched. With perfect calm and not even a pause in her movement, she said, "He had the press, I believe." She spun once more and finished in a deep curtsey, then straightened and began stripping off her exercise suit. "I'm going to swim. Will you come with me?"

She threw herself into the Heliomere without looking back. After a bit, I undressed and followed. Compared to the chill of the air, the water felt boiling hot. The heat drew out the last of my anger, though. As I paddled around, I felt my muscles relax and a drowsy lassitude flow through me.

Too soon, it seemed, Selene shouted, "Don't go to sleep, Gordy. It's time to get out."

We made the cold dash across the beach to the cabin, picking up our clothes on the way. Inside, we huddled together wishing for a fire and toweled ourselves dry while the polycarpet ran rainbows of browns and electric blues around our feet. In the course of it, I got my arms around Selene. I pulled her against me. She met my mouth hungrily, but when I started pulling her toward the fake animal pelt in front of the fireplace, she rammed me with a sharp hip bone and wiggled loose.

"I don't have time. I have to dry my hair before I wake Mandy."

"You never have time for anything but exercising," I complained. "Will you ever?"

She licked her lips. "Ask me in January."

I walked back up the beach wondering in bemusement if I could be falling in love with two such different women at the same time. If so, how fortunate they were the same woman.

I called Amanda later. I expected to find her herself, yesterday already forgotten, but she still sounded anxious. "Matthew, can you come up?"

I looked unhappily at the couple standing in the outer office with Caro. What a time for clients to walk in. "I have some people here. Can it possibly wait?"

There was a pause while she debated. "I suppose so, but, please, come when you can."

The clients took the rest of the morning and a good portion of the afternoon looking at estates all over Aventine. A sale of the size property they were interested in would bring a huge commission, too big for me to risk seeming preoccupied or impatient. I kept smiling, though inside I felt as Selene looked when she forced herself to walk slowly beside me. I even took them back to the cabletrain, but I had no sooner seen them off than I flung myself back into the runabout and drove up to Amanda's cabin.

"What's wrong?" I asked anxiously, walking in.

She sat wrapped in a shawl, staring into the empty fireplace. The polychair had turned pale gray. "She's trying to take over, Matthew."

I pulled another chair up beside her and sat down. "What do you mean?"

She clutched the shawl tighter around her. "When I got up this morning, that chair you're sitting in was bright blue. It's always brown or yellow for you. Selene has to have been sitting in it."

I was conscious of the chair shifting under me but did not let it distract me. "Does that mean she's taking over?"

Amanda laced and unlaced her fingers in her lap. "In the past, there's sometimes been reason for her to come out of time, some errand I can't do or a need to write me a message. There's no note this time. I also found damp towels that weren't there last night. If she isn't honoring our agreement any longer, soon it won't be minutes she's taking; it will be hours, then days, until there's no time left I can count on for my own. I don't know what to do, Matthew. How can I fight her?" She looked up pleadingly.

I took a breath. What could I say to that? "I know a psychiatrist who spends her weekends here in Aventine. Perhaps she can help."

"No!" Amanda jumped up, hands white knuckled on the edges of her shawl. "She'd only want to reintegrate me."

I stood, too, and cupped her face between my hands. "Would that be so terrible? Then all the time would be yours."

"But—I'd—I'd have to become part of—what Selene is." She pulled away from me, shaking her head. "That's unthinkable. I couldn't bear it. There's no other way but to go on as I am. So promise me, Matthew, promise that if you ever see Selene, you'll tell me. I have to know when she's stealing time."

I never wanted to lie to her, but I did, and with a straight face. "I promise."

Amanda walked into my arms and buried her face against my neck. "Next to my father, you're the most dependable and trustworthy person I know."

If I looked as guilty as I felt, I thanked the stars she could not see my face just now.

She stirred in my arms. I felt a ripple of tension in her body. She lifted her head and kissed me hard. I grabbed her shoulders and held her off at arm's length to look at her.

"Selene," I hissed. "What are you doing here?"

"I sensed you felt the two of us ought to talk." She slipped out of my hands and went to curl up in one of the chairs.

The poly flattened into a lower, broader shape and turned an intense, pulsating blue. It looked odd to see Selene in Amanda's clothes, but odder still to find that despite them, she looked like herself and not Amanda.

Energy ran like a restless, self-willed thing under her skin. She could not even sit without that coiled-spring tension.

"Talk," she said.

"I'd intended to do it tomorrow. What am I supposed to tell Amanda when she comes back?"

"If we take the same positions, she'll never know she was gone. By the way, thanks for saying nothing about me."

"Next time I'll tell her. I won't lie to her again. So I guess this will all have to stop."

She frowned. "You mean quit running together?"

"I mean quit everything: running, swimming, practicing—all of it. You shouldn't come again until January, when you're supposed to."

"Quit *practicing?*" Her topaz eyes flared. "I can't afford to stop practicing." She leaned toward me. "Gordy, it's time she doesn't *use*. She hasn't missed it before, and if I'm careful not to let her catch me out again, she'll never miss it."

I shook my head. "You're breaking an agreement."

"I'm not taking over, though. You know that's just a paranoid fantasy. I use only enough time for practice and no more. I don't even practice as much as I should. I go six whole months without taking class even once. Do you know what not taking class does to dancers?"

"Yet you're continuously aware. In a sense, you already have more than your share of time."

She snorted. "You think continuous awareness is a good thing? You have no idea what it's like being locked up in her head, seeing and hearing everything but able to do nothing. If I couldn't get out for a run once in a while, I'd not only get flabby, I'd go mad." She bounced out of the chair and came over to lace her fingers together behind my neck. "What about you? It's three months until January. How can I give up seeing you for three whole months?"

I did not like that idea, either, but— "What else can we do? Shall I lie to Amanda and hate you for making me do it?"

She winced. "No."

"We'll be able to see each other all we like in January."

"January." She groaned the word. "That's forever. Kiss me good-bye, then; give me a memory to keep with me."

Kissing Selene was like grabbing a high-voltage wire. The charge in her swept through us both. I could almost smell the smoke from my sizzling nerve endings. And this time when I pushed her onto the pelt before the fireplace, she did not resist.

I came out of postcoital drowsiness to realize that my nerves had not been cauterized, after all. They recognized that the room was chilling. Selene was already fastening her dress. I groped halfheartedly for my clothes.

"This would be a nice night for a fire. Shall I build one?" I asked.

Her hair had come loose during the lovemaking and hung down over her face. She parted it to look at me. My breathing stopped. Goldstone, not topaz, fixed on me. In a voice of such preternatural calm it terrified me, Amanda said, "Who were you talking to?"

I could not answer with ice in my chest, only stare back while she hunted around for her hairpins.

"I do hope you aren't going to say it was to me, not with a chair adapted to Selene right beside you."

Wordlessly, I crawled into my pants.

She found her hairpins. Sitting down in the same chair Selene had occupied, she swept her hair up with her arms, then used one hand to hold it while she began pinning it in place. The poly turned a bright mottle of yellow and orange.

"I checked the clock," she said.

Her voice faltered only a little, but her hands began to shake. The orange in the chair's color went darker and the yellows bled away. Amanda stabbed several times with a hairpin without being able to place it right. After the seventh or eighth try, she stood up, letting the hairpins spill on to the carpet. She walked to the far end of the fireplace, where she stood with her back to me, toying with the tops of the fire tools.

"It hasn't been long at all since—since I told you I trusted you."

That hurt. I climbed to my feet and reached out to touch her shoulder. "I was talking to her for your sake."

She whirled. *"My* sake? Matthew, please don't lie to me again." Tears hung on her voice.

I ran a hand through my hair. "I'm not lying. I was arguing that Selene shouldn't use any of your time."

"It was a very—short argument." Her voice caught. "And I find the—conclusion rather—inconsistent." Her control slipped. Tears spilled out of the goldstone eyes, and her hand showed white on the handle of the tool caddy.

Guilt and pain tore at me. I chased through my head for something to comfort her. "Mandy, I—"

I bit my tongue but too late. She shrieked like a stricken animal and came at me swinging the poker.

I backed away, throwing my arms up to protect my head. Amanda might not be athletic, but she had all her released emotion and Selene's sinewy gymnastic strength behind that swing. What probably saved my life was that she did not have Selene's conscious co-ordination. The poker only brushed my forearm before smashing into the stone of the fireplace.

But I forgot to watch out for the rebound. Pain lanced up my arm. I went down, bouncing my head off the edge of the raised hearth as I fell.

Amanda screamed again. I tried to roll sideways, but my body would not respond, and I steeled myself for the second, almost surely fatal blow. It never came, though. Instead, something dropped to the floor with a loud *thud*. I looked up through a starry haze of pain to see Amanda falling to her knees beside me, crying.

"Matthew—Matthew, I'm sorry. I didn't mean to hurt you." Her hand stroked my forehead. "It was the name you called me. I hate that name. Selene calls me that. I hit out at the name. I know this wasn't your fault. Selene did it."

I tried to shake my head, but it hurt like hell. Something like silver foil wrapped around the edges of my vision, too. "Selene isn't the evil genius you think, Amanda." My voice sounded whisper weak in my ears.

Amanda's tears splashed on my face. "Don't defend her. She's just like her mother, and my father told me what *she* was. Selene's been after my time ever since her mother died. Now she wants everything that makes my time worth living, too." She clutched her hands together, lacing and unlacing the fingers.

Appalled, I stared up at her. This kind of thinking had lain behind her madonna's serenity? "You can't really believe that!"

"She probably let me catch the two of you making love so I'd throw you out and she could have you to herself." Amanda sat back hugging herself as though cold. "I know what she's doing, but I don't know what to do to stop her. If she were a disease, I could take drugs against her. If she were a cancer, I could cut her out. How do I cure myself of this—this parasite of the mind?"

She stood, using an arm of a chair to help push herself to her feet. From where her hand touched, livid streamers of orange and scarlet radiated out across the surface of the poly. A marbled pool of the same colors spread from her feet into the carpet. She stood with her eyes searching the cabin as though expecting it to give her an answer. Her gaze fixed on the kitchen.

"Cut her out," she said.

She ran for the kitchen, her feet leaving a path like bloody stepping stones.

"Amanda!" I called.

I tried to sit up, but my head weighed a thousand kilos. I managed to roll on to my side and as though looking down a silver tunnel, watched Amanda jerk open a drawer. She reached in. I gritted my teeth against the nausea the effort of moving brought and lurched onto my hands and knees.

Her hand came out of the drawer with a thin knife. *"Amanda!"* I crawled toward the kitchen, dragging the weight of my head. "Amanda, what are you doing?"

The arm injured by the poker gave way, dropping my head and shoulders on to the carpet. The shock sent a new wave of nausea through me and muffled my vision and hearing in black velvet.

I could not have been out more than moments. When my sight cleared, I was staring into polycarpet turned murky green. I heard the soft whisper of crushing pile; then a tide of scarlet and purple eddied against the edge of my green.

"I can cut her out, Matthew," Amanda said from above me. She spoke in a voice that sounded low but trembled on the edge of hysteria. "She only comes to dance. I read once about a horse whose tendons were cut just a little, but he never was able to race again."

"My god!" I could see her feet and, by rolling on to my back, look up at her rising above me toward the beams of the roof, but I could not move. My head seemed nailed to the floor. The knife gleamed in her hand. "Selene," I called. "I can't reach her! Help me!"

Amanda cried, "Matthew, don't—" Her eyes widened with horror. Her mouth moved again.

But this time, Selene's voice, firm and brisk, spoke. "I think we'd better have a talk, Mandy."

With another twist of facial features, Amanda said in a rising voice, "You can't do this, Selene. You're cheating."

"I can't let you ruin my dancing career."

"It's the only way I know to make you go away and leave me alone."

Amanda backed as she spoke until a wall stopped her. The polycarpet extending up the surface responded to her touch with an exploding aurora of hot oranges, reds, and violets. "I've tried living with you, Selene, but it doesn't work. Now I won't have anything more to do with you!"

"You have no choice. Unfortunately, neither do I." The colors cooled as Selene spoke. Tendrils of green and blue wormed their way into the pattern. "I'm as much a part of this body as you are. Hamstring me and we'll both be crippled for life."

Scarlet wiped out the blues and green. Amanda cried, "Let's see!"

She swooped toward her ankles with the knife. The long skirt of her dress hung in the way. Before she could pick up the hem, her left hand stiffened.

"No!" She screamed in rage and terror. "Selene, let go of my hand!"

Behind the left shoulder, the polycarpet turned bright blue. The left hand reached for the wrist of the hand with the knife.

Amanda wrenched herself sideways, stabbing at the left hand. "Leave me alone!"

The left hand dodged. "You don't seem to understand, Mandy. I can't. We're joined indissolubly, till death us do part," Selene said.

"All right."

The knife turned toward her own chest. Selene's hand leaped to intercept, closing on Amanda's wrist. Amanda screamed inarticulately. Her whole body convulsed with the effort to tear loose. Selene held on. Slowly, Selene twisted the wrist back and down while the polycarpet around them swirled in wave after wave of color pulsating with every labored breath of the struggling body. The maelstrom spread out across the floor and up the walls, even affecting the chairs so that they, too, raged with color and pulsed to the time of Amanda's breathing.

Amanda's wrist bent farther. Her fingers fought to hold on to the knife, but with each moment they loosened more. She sobbed. "I'm going to kill you, Selene. Sooner or later, I'll kill you!"

"No, Mandy." Selene's voice came through clenched teeth. "I won't allow that. I always know what you're thinking. And I won't retire. You'll just have to live with me as always."

"I won't! I can't bear it!" Amanda wailed as the knife dropped from her fingers.

Selene sent it out of reach with a swift kick of her left foot. "You'll have to learn."

"Selene," I said, "don't push too hard."

Amanda looked wild, her eyes darting around like those of a trapped animal.

"You're stuck, Mandy," Selene said. "There's no way out."

"No, no, no, no!"

The desperation in Amanda's voice terrified me. "Selene, stop it!"

But she went on relentlessly, deaf to me. "We have to live together all our lives no matter how much you hate it, no matter if it means meeting my friends and hearing what your body has been doing while I controlled it. Because it *is* your body, always. You're a part of me, and I of you."

Amanda whimpered and fell silent.

The next moment, Selene, wholly Selene, stood there. She hurried across the room to kneel beside me. "You've got blood all over your head."

I grabbed her wrist as she reached to touch me. "Never mind me. How is Amanda?"

She snapped her wrist loose and stood. "You need a doctor." She turned toward the phone.

"What about Amanda?"

Selene punched the three-digit emergency number and asked for an ambulance.

"Selene, *where is Amanda?*"

Selene hung up the phone. "She's gone."

"Gone?" I sat bolt upright. A wave of dizziness knocked me flat again. "How can she be gone?"

"It was an intolerable situation for her. She went catatonic to escape."

Relief flooded me. "Then she's still alive."

"But I can't reach her. She won't respond to anything I do."

"Haven't you done enough?" I sighed. "When I called you, I didn't mean for you to push her like that. Couldn't you guess what she might do? We'll call my psychiatrist friend and have her help bring Amanda back."

Selene moved around the room, touching the chairs, working her bare feet through the carpet, soothing away the bizarre reflections of the struggle. Gradually, the chairs and carpet softened to a uniform blue.

"Selene, did you hear me?"

She stopped moving. "I heard."

"Then will you call my friend?" I asked impatiently.

She did not move or answer.

Cold gripped me. "Selene!"

She looked down at me with clouded topaz eyes. "I'll—think about it."

Broken Stairways, Walls of Time

IOOOUOOOOOOOOOOOOOOOOO

I never think of Aventine without remembering Cybele Bournais. Once, years ago, we were lovers there. We lived together for ten unforgettable months, over a spring and a summer into winter, until my holosymphony *Summer and Cybele* took us our separate ways to fame. She lingers in my memory more clearly than in any holo album. I see her on the broken stairways of her Treehouse, beyond the walls of time grown up between us, forever young, forever golden voiced. I choose not to remember how our last meeting ended except to wonder from time to time what malicious caprice of fate could have wanted to bring us together again, then asked such a price for the meeting.

I was not thinking of Cybele when I came back to Aventine. I was looking at architecture. My new holosymphony was to be about the personalities of houses, and Aventine overflowed with homes of great character. Even twenty-five years ago, when the stargate had just been built above Gateside on Diana Mountain and Aventine was principally an artists' colony, not the retreat of the rich and famous it is now, eccentrics had been living there. They built highly individual, often bizarre houses. Days when the feverish pitch of our creativity faltered and no one felt like hanging around the young Xhosar Kain's studio or walking down to Jessica Vanier's cabin on Birch Cove, we would go house watching. We could kill an afternoon staring at Taj Mahals and Norman castles, pseudo-Frank Lloyd Wrights, and constructions that defied

66

ready classification. And I understood from Margo Chen, my agent in Gateside, that now there were even more and stranger houses.

I had the chance to discover first-hand how right she was. Because I was not sure what I would find, I did not let Margo hire anyone to approach the owners. Using a rented car, I drove around Aventine looking at the houses myself and personally asking permission to tape them. Some owners refused, but most offered complete cooperation, flattered to have the famous Simon Doyle asking to include their houses in a holosymphony.

And so it was that early one afternoon I drove the car up the pine-lined drive of the house that twenty-five years before we had named the Treehouse. It was not in a tree but tree shaped. From a ground-level reception hall, half a dozen stairways swept upward like great branches through clear plastic tubes. Along the graceful arabesques, rooms blossomed like flowers.

I stopped the car. Even from the driveway I could see the house had aged. Yellow discolored the plastic of the stair tubes. On several of the higher flights, the carpeting had become threadbare. I could see gaping holes left where treads and risers had torn loose. Tangled and overgrown lawns surrounded it. I got out of the car wondering how the owners of the neighboring estates tolerated this derelict in their midst. I had seen no other house in Aventine in such a state of disrepair. Perhaps it survived because it could not be seen from the road.

I walked under the stairways and around the house, staring up at the room platforms. The drapes inside the transparent walls were closed, but the sag of several in upper rooms suggested more neglect. I pictured the furniture thick with dust. Was the house abandoned? If so, how could I contact the owner? I certainly wanted to use it in my holosymphony. If anything, its seedy appearance only strengthened its character.

"Excuse me," a voice said behind me, "but this is

private property. Unless you have business, I must ask you to leave."

For a moment, I was frozen. I knew only one voice in the world that could sound so polite, so warm with life and laughter, yet carry a threatening edge of steel. I turned and looked down into fondly remembered jade eyes.

Cybelle Bournais still looked like the thin, heart-high girl I had known twenty-five years before. Her jade-green hair still hung loose about her, a silky cape long enough to sit on. And she still appeared to like those high-necked body suits that fit like a coat of paint. Today she wore black.

"Cybele, this is a wonderful surprise," I said.

The jade eyes regarded me without recognition.

I frowned. "Surely I haven't changed that much. I'm Simon Doyle."

She looked thoughtful. "Just a moment." She disappeared.

I stared at the spot where she had vanished. I wondered again, as I often had before, if she were entirely human. She had appeared suddenly one winter, a no one from nowhere, just a diminutive girl with a starvation appetite and a magic voice. Lord, that voice! It was all she needed. It was a fine musical instrument she played with consummate skill. She built visions for us, made flowers in the snow and comets at noon— moved us to any emotion she desired. In the beginning, she sang in bars in Gateside, and when she could not find work, she lived with one or another of us in Aventine. She could always find someone willing to give her a bed for a night or a week or even for several months, as I had.

Cybele reappeared. This time she wore a metallic red body suit, and her hair was pulled back in a long horse tail. "Simon, of course I recognize you." Her voice caught the fresh gold of a spring dawn. "I never expected to see you here."

I realized then what was happening. This was not actually Cybele but a holographic image. The first one had been a recording, triggered by my presence, to warn me away. When my response fell outside its program, it had been replaced by another that could deal with me. But why a second holo, I wondered?

"Cybele, are you back behind your watchdog somewhere?"

The holo regarded me a moment, then smiled. "Yes."

"Why the puppet show? Come down and see me yourself." I peered up at the house, trying to find the room she might be in.

"You must allow me my fun, Simon." Her voice tickled like a lash with a feather tied to the end. "You instigated my fascination with holography, you know. I think it was why I married Eldon."

I remembered hearing she had married Eldon Kliest, the computer king, and remembered, too, that he had died in a hovercraft accident. That had been nearly six years earlier.

"What brings you to the Treehouse?" Cybele asked through the holo.

"I could say I've come courting a widow, but the truth is I'm working on a new composition. How long have you lived here?"

"Since my husband died." The holo lifted a brow. "I know the rest of you laughed at it, but I've always loved this house. Women look so graceful on stairways." The holo turned toward the front door. "Come in."

With a click, the door swung open. "Enter, please," the holo said, and disappeared.

Inside, the reception hall did not repeat the derelict look of the outside. The black-and-white tile had a mirror polish, reflecting bright tapestries and paintings hung between the stairways. The door closed behind me. As it shut, another holo appeared in one of the stairway entrances. This one was of Cybele, too, but her hair had been dyed black and cut chin length. She wore a linen dress and an elaborate Egyptian headdress.

"This way," she said.

I followed her up the stairs.

"How do you like my costume?"

"It's from *Cleopatra*, isn't it?"

"You recognize it." Cybele sounded pleased. "Did you ever see"—she blinked out of existence as we turned a bend in the stairs but reappeared a moment later and continued talking as if there had been no interruption—"the show? I sang in it for almost five years." She began one of its songs that she had helped make popular. Her voice wrapped around me as magically as ever. She broke off as we reached a door a dizzying distance above the ground. "Go on in."

I pushed open the door and went in.

"Hello, Simon."

Cybele sat curled in a huge basket chair at the far end of the sitting room. I started toward her but stopped short at the sight of two black leopards lounging around the bottom of the chair. One of them lifted its head and snarled.

Cybele smiled at my fear. "They won't hurt you, Simon. Sit down anywhere."

I eyed the leopards and found a leather chair at what I hoped was a prudent distance away.

Cybele arched a brow, then shrugged. "Tell me everything that's happened to you since we saw each other last."

"You tell me about you," I replied.

"Your work is so much more fascinating. I've been one of your most faithful collectors. Did you know that? I have everything you've ever done. This is my favorite, of course."

I did not see her move, but suddenly the sitting room became a summer mountain meadow. Flowers grew at my feet. They looked real enough to pick, and though I could not smell them, I found myself remembering the scent that had hung sweet and heavy in the meadow the day we taped. Music swelled into the opening theme from *Summer and Cybele*.

I listened critically. It could have been better. I wished I had had the ability of the current computers when I was synthesizing the sound for the holosymphony.

A small figure in white came running up the meadow toward me. In moments, Cybele dropped,

laughing, into the flowers at my feet, and the sound-
track began the first strains of the theme Paul Mc-
Cartney later set to words for her as "I Am Summer."

The meadow returned to being a sitting room. Cybele smiled at me. "Where are you staying?"

"I have a hotel room in Gateside."

"Gateside?" She frowned. "But that means an
hour's ride over on the cabletrain every morning and
an hour back at night."

I shrugged. "Without hotels in Aventine, there's
nothing else to do."

She looked at me. "I have fourteen bedrooms I
don't use."

"Above the broken stairs?"

"Mostly below. My rooms are above."

My brows went up. "Your rooms? Cybele, those
stairs look dangerous."

Her expression remained placid, but a smile flickered in her voice. "It does insure privacy."

I stared at her. Since when had Cybele Bournais,
keep-me-in-the-center Cybele, wanted privacy? Or
gone to such measures to guard it?

But after that my protests became token. This was
an ideal base for taping. I could reach any house I
wanted in a matter of minutes. I could even walk in
some instances. And in the evening, I would have the
company of a fascinating woman I had once passion-
ately desired and almost loved. I wanted very much
to learn how much she had changed, too, and why. I
gave in to her.

She nodded as though she had expected nothing
else. Standing, she started for the door. "We'll tour
the house, and you can pick the room you like best."

With yawns and stretches, the panthers rose to follow her.

I bit my lip. "Are they coming, too?"

She laughed back over her shoulder. "I told you,
they won't hurt you."

One of the panthers passed by me so close its tail
touched my leg. I could not feel it, though. Nor could
I smell the animal, I realized.

"They're holos, aren't they?"

Cybele nodded. A panther rubbed against her leg. She stroked the huge black head.

I frowned. The big cats might be very realistic, but holos could not be touched.

"This way, Simon."

As she passed through the door, I saw without surprise that she disappeared momentarily.

"And you're another." Only holos could touch other holos.

She turned around. Her voice flung that feather-tipped lash at me again. "It took you long enough to realize it. This one is very good, don't you think?"

I sighed. "What kind of game are you playing?"

She smiled. "Showing an old lover he isn't the only one who can play with holos."

"When do I see the real you?"

"Soon enough. Indulge me a while longer. Now come see my Treehouse."

The holo showed me through the house. We climbed the sweeps of its stair branches, looked into the fourteen vacant bedrooms, saw sitting rooms and game rooms, checked the dining room. The holo, whom I privately dubbed the Panther Lady, moved with such naturalness and reacted so appropriately to me and the house, even making subtle changes in facial expression, that it was hard to remember this was just an image, not a living woman. But around our feet prowled the panthers, which occasionally walked through my legs, and the Panther Lady did disappear at points along the stairs and as we went through doorways. That served to remind me of her unreality.

In one room we tripped an automatic holo. She appeared before the fireplace in a gold body suit, her hair striped orange and red. "Welcome," she said. "This game room is appointed with—" She broke off. When she resumed a moment later, her voice had changed from hostess polite to a more natural tone. "This is Lady Sunshine, from *Suddenly Spring*. Pardon me for not shutting her down before you arrived. When you wander around on your own, you'll find others like her. They're there to explain the facilities of each room."

Lady Sunshine smiled, curtsied, and was turned off.

We did see other holos. Once we met Cleopatra again and, for a few moments before Cybele turned her off, a woman on the stairs in Tudor dress. I recognized Anne Boleyn as Cybele had played her in Kyle Rogers' musical *Anne*.

I finally chose a bedroom low on a solid flight of stairs and drove back to the town square to catch the late-afternoon cabletrain back to Gateside for my equipment. By midnight, I was back and installed in the Treehouse. Cleopatra met me in the reception hall, but she gave only programmed responses to questions I asked. The rest of the house lay dark and silent.

I woke in the morning to find a short-haired Cybele in a green jerkin and hose sitting curled on the foot of my bed. A fairy fluttered over her head. I slid a foot toward her. It passed under her without obstruction.

"So that's how you looked playing Peter Pan," I said.

The holo laughed. "You're very clever, Simon. When you're up, come over to the dining room for breakfast."

"Are you going to be there?"

She regarded me for a moment with glittering jade eyes. "Oh, yes. Don't be too long or everything will be cold." Laughing, she and Tinkerbell winked out.

I did indeed find Cybele in the dining room. I found dozens of her there, surely every holo manifestation of her in her computer: Cleopatra, Anne Boleyn, Lady Sunshine, the Panther Lady, and many Cybeles in costumes I could not identify. Even the panthers were there, and a pair of magnificent leopards, prowling majestically among the Cybeles. The holos all talked at each other.

I stood awed by the thought of the program necessary to handle this many conversations—until I listened more closely. Except for an occasional punch line of a joke or anecdote, the "conversations" consisted mainly of continuous repetitions of: "Mumble, murmur, chatter, mumble."

That discovered, I began wondering how to find

breakfast in this mob. Then Cybele's voice called above the noise of her Doppelgängers. "I'm here, Simon."

The question was where, but I had no desire to chase her through a crowd of phantoms. "I don't have time for games this morning. I'm sorry. I hope I can see you this evening."

I turned and started to leave.

The noise stopped with a suddenness that left a vacuum. I looked back. The holos had all vanished. I was alone with the long table and a woman at the far end, jade haired in a jade-green body suit and wide belt of knotted gold cords.

She arched her brows and slid her fingers over the knots of her belt. "How serious you've become." Her voice carried a light sting.

Cybele, if it was really she this time, looked less hungry than the girl I had lived with but otherwise little changed by the years. I started toward her to take a closer look.

"Sit down and eat your breakfast," she said.

I eyed her. "Are you real?"

For answer, she picked an orange from a bowl in front of her and tossed it at me. I fully expected my fingers to close through it, but when I caught the fruit, it was solid, with volume and weight—real.

Cybele's fingers played across her belt. "I have to work today, too."

"Cybele—" I began.

But she rose and swept past me out of the room.

I wished I could tape her house that day so I could track her from room to room and talk to her, but I had another house already scheduled. I ate, collected my cameras, and left.

The house I had scheduled took all day. Cut into the cliffs above the long, winding length of the Lunamere, the house made exterior shots difficult. I had to tape with a telephoto lens from points to each side along the cliffs and from a boat below. It was late afternoon before exterior and interior taping was finished.

I came back to the Treehouse in the early evening to find it ablaze with light and music and alive with holos moving up and down the stairs. Cleopatra attended the reception hall. When I asked for Cybele, she led me up to a sitting room.

Cybele sat in a large easy chair before a lighted fireplace at the far end, leopards lounging at her feet. She watched a holo of herself seated on a tall stool in the middle of the room, singing. I recognized both the song and holo as being from an album she made not long after leaving Aventine.

I coughed. Cybele's eyes switched from holo to me. The girl on the stool vanished.

"Ah, Simon, you're back." Her voice had a delight that sent an old warmth through me.

I started for her chair, intending to kiss her, but Cybele frowned, and the leopards lifted their heads, snarling. I knew they were only holos, but I stopped, Cybele's message clear. It puzzled and disturbed me. Cybele used to like being touched and shown affection. She had craved it.

As though she sensed the questions in me, Cybele drew farther back into her chair. She toyed with the knots of her belt. "I hope you had a good day."

I considered asking her outright what was wrong. The Cybele of old, however, had been adamant in refusing to talk about things she had not volunteered, and I did not think that that had changed. I let the questions run around unasked inside me. "I'll know how good when I replay the tapes. Would you like to see them?"

Her face lighted. "I would. Thank you."

The fire went out. The leopards followed us down and across to my room, though, and stretched out at her feet again when she sat down in a chair near the door.

"Why don't you stand over here near me?" I asked.

She smiled. "I'm sure I'll be able to see just as well from here."

If she had not remained undisturbed by passing through doorways and I had not felt her body heat and smelled her perfume as we walked, I might have wondered if she were Cybele, after all, or only another of Cybele's holos. I toyed with the thought, then pushed it aside as I fed the tapes into my computer.

"There's no sound right now, of course. I won't synthesize that until I have my visual sequences the way I want them."

"I remember."

The bedroom became part of the Grotto, with lamps and planters attached to stalactites and with stalagmites rising from the floor to support tables and couches. A wall entirely of glass looked out over the cobalt waters of the Lunamere.

"So that's what it looks like inside," Cybele said. "Remember how much time we spent wondering? What fun you must be having finding out if our guesses were right or not."

I had to admit I enjoyed the taping. "Tomorrow should be even better. I'm doing the pink Sugar Plum Castle on Star Circle. Why don't you come with me?"

"Thank you, but I almost never go out."

I shut off the tape with a stab of my finger. Cybele sat with her chin bowed, her jade hair obscuring her face.

"You make personal appearances, don't you?"

She shook her head. "I even tape my albums here. I have a recording studio upstairs."

I could not believe this. Cybele Bournais—a *recluse?* "But you've always loved crowds and traveling."

She shrugged. "People change. I'm afraid I'm keeping you from your work. I'll see you later."

She left, trailed by the holo leopards.

But, in fact, she hardly saw me later. We had dinner seated at opposite ends of the long table with holo Cybeles lining both sides between us. After dinner, we climbed to the sitting room with the fireplace. Cleopatra and Peter Pan went with us, chattering in simultaneous but unrelated conversations about Mark Anthony and Never-Never Land. In the sitting room, Cybele touched the keys imbedded in the arm of her big chair by the fireplace and filled the room with *Summer and Cybele.*

She made it impossible to come anywhere near her

that night. In the morning, I had to share breakfast with the leopards and panthers as well as Cybele. I had spent the night thinking, however, and I had a carrot I hoped would tempt her closer.

"I'm putting off the Sugar Plum Castle until another day and taping the Treehouse today."

She straightened in her chair, jade eyes glittering. "May I watch?"

I had been hoping she would ask. "Of course."

And, in fact, it did bring her out. She still kept a distance between us, but less than the night before, as she followed me everywhere. She watched in fascination as I taped from every possible angle in every room and stairway. When I caught her in the frame, she did not appear to mind at all.

I dangled another carrot. "How would you like to be the subject of another holosymphony? We could call it *Encore: Cybele*."

She bit her lip and looked down. "It wouldn't be the same, Simon. Repeats never are. That's why I never renew a relationship with a man once it's over." She looked at me through her jade hair. "You were hoping to take up where we left off, weren't you?"

Not really, though the idea had occurred to me.

"It's out of the question." She played her voice, making it curl around me soft and warm as a kitten, then sting like a lash. "I wouldn't want to spoil my memories of our time together before."

"There's more to it than that." I felt, strangely, angry as well as concerned. She was half lying, evading, throwing phantoms up between us. I set down my camera and started up the staircase to where she stood slightly above me. "You won't even shake hands. What is it? Why are you so afraid to be touched? Are you real or just another holo, after all?"

She fled away from me, up one flight after another, up the broken stairways. I tried to follow, but the gaping hole made by missing treads stopped me. I could not imagine how Cybele had climbed this way. She must have, though; I saw her above me, in one last glimpse of jade hair and green body suit, before the door of her room slammed between us.

I stood for some time watching the door of her room high above me. It remained closed. After a while, I went down to a sitting room and called Margo in Gateside.

"Tell me about Cybele Bournais."

Margo's voice came back drily over the wire. "My dear Simon, what can I possibly tell you that you haven't already learned for yourself long ago?"

"When did she become a recluse?"

"Oh—that. She was in the hovercraft accident with her husband. Afterwards she disappeared for nearly a year. Rumor said she was in Switzerland, having her face rebuilt. When she came back, she bought that incredible house and locked herself in. She makes all her albums and media appearances there. She's never turned away visitors. That's something odd. She even throws large parties up there, but her agent tells me she refuses personal-appearance offers every week. If you find out anything, do let me know. I'm dying of curiosity."

I was in the process of hanging up when she added, "Keep out of high rooms today. There's a thunderstorm here that's a good preview of apocalypse, and it's headed your way."

I glanced out the window. Purple-gray clouds were boiling across the sky, burying the blue.

I hung up and hurried back to my camera. I did not want to miss the chance to tape the house in changing weather. Not until several minutes later did it register that as I laid down the receiver, there had been not one click of disconnection on the other end but two. Cybele must have listened in on my conversation with Margo.

The wind began rising. I could feel it pushing at the stairways. The sky became a dark tent, sagging in waterlogged bulges overhead. Soon flickers of lightning were chasing across the bulges.

I forgot the Treehouse and pointed my holocamera at the sky. Somewhere, sometime, I might need some footage of a storm, and this one promised to be very dramatic.

The first thunder reached me, sound followed by an answering shiver of the stairway tube.

"Simon."

I looked up to see Cybele coming down the stairs toward me. For a moment, I thought her hair streamed in the rising wind, but it was only rippling caused by the motion of her descent. She halted seven or eight steps from me.

"Don't pry into my life." Her voice cracked like a bolt of lightning, echoing the flashes overhead.

"I'm not trying to pry. I'm concerned about you."

Her hands bit into the knots of her belt. "You're curious. There's a difference. I invited you to stay because I was once happy living with you and wanted to see you again, but if you meddle in matters that don't concern you, I'll have to ask you to leave." Lightning glared on her face, striking sparks from her jade eyes.

I sighed. "All right. I leave you to live your life as you choose, but I wish—"

I never had the chance to tell her I wished she would tell me what had made her change. From the corner of my eye, I saw lightning arc from the clouds down to the mountain below us. The lights along the stairs went out.

I whistled. "That one hit a power line. Do you have candles? We'd better light some."

By flashes of lightning, I saw Cybele staring at me in horror. She clutched at her belt.

"Candles?" I repeated.

For the second time that day, she fled away from me up the broken stairways to her room. And again I followed, trying to remember exactly where the breaks were so I would not fall in. I could see enough by the frequent lightning to find my way after her. Strangely, I saw no breaks. I found myself just a few steps below her door without having seen any of the holes in the stairs.

I looked back behind me. The stairs dropped away, whole and sound. Suddenly, I understood. The broken sections were holographic illusions. When the electricity in the house went off, so had the holos. I whirled to stare up at Cybele's door. More holos. What was real and how much holo in this house? And why?

I made the last few steps in two bounds and knocked on her door. "Cybele, open the door."

There was no response from inside.

I knocked again. "Cybele, answer me."

I heard something inside but not a voice. It sounded like metal scraping over metal.

I pounded. "Are you all right, Cybele?"

There was only that scraping sound. Then I heard her panting.

I tried the door. Not surprisingly, it was locked. I peered at the lock. It looked intended to be more of a reminder than a deterrent to anyone wanting in. I raised a foot and gave it a hard kick.

The door opened in a crash of splintering wood and screech of metal. Inside, by the light of an oil lamp, I saw Cybele whirl from a piece of equipment.

I looked around the room. It must be the studio she mentioned. It was packed with recording equipment and computer elements. What I saw was capable of running all the holos in the house and then some. And the piece before Cybele was a battery-powered generator. The oil lamp sat on top of it, lighting her work.

"Your auxiliary power is out, too? May I help you there?" I asked.

She pointed the screwdriver she held toward the door. "Get out."

She was obviously speaking. Her lips moved, and the sound came from her direction, but I did not recognize the voice. Not even in moments of greatest stress had Cybele ever used a high-pitched rasp like that.

I stared at her in disbelief. "Cybele?"

Over our heads, rain suddenly drummed on the roof. Thunder boomed.

Cybele glared at me with the eyes of a trapped animal. "Yes, I'm Cybele. Now get out of my house."

The words were rough, the syllables broken, without any of the rich beauty and control Cybele was famous for, but they carried more hate than I had ever heard in a human voice before. The hand not holding the screwdriver fumbled for her belt, stopped, and went to her throat.

Then I understood. This was Cybele's real voice. The one I had been hearing these past few days came from the computer. She controlled it through the knotted gold belt she was always touching.

"What happened?" I asked.

She looked down so her long jade hair fell forward over her face. The noise of thunder and rain made her voice almost inaudible. I strained to catch even a few words. ". . . crushed my throat in the hovercraft accident."

Surgeons and cosmetisculpture could rebuild a face but not restore something as delicate as a voice. I fought down a wave of pity. I did not want to pity her. Actually, what she had now was not a bad voice. Its hoarseness might even have been attractive in another woman, but Cybele had had something so remarkable, so beautiful, that anything less seemed grotesquely ugly.

"So you've been synthesizing your voice for speaking and singing the past five years. You've done a spectacular job. I couldn't come anywhere near it."

It certainly explained many things about her behavior. She had to remain near her computer in order to talk.

Cybele tossed her hair back. Her eyes were those of a tigress. She came at me with the screwdriver in both hands, like a dagger.

It was so sudden she almost drove the blade into my neck before I realized what she was doing. I grabbed for her arms. The blade scraped my forearm.

"Cybele, stop that! What do you think I'm going to do, tell the world about you? I won't."

I had hold of her wrists, but I could not twist the screwdriver out of her grip. Anger gave her incredible strength. The blade dug into my other forearm as she struggled to pull free. I used all my strength to lift her off her feet and throw her backward, away from me.

She hit the front of the auxiliary generator. The oil

lamp on top rocked once and fell forward. It shattered as it hit the floor.

I yelled a warning and leaped to pull Cybele aside, but she jerked away from me, and the sheet of flame went up between us. In seconds, the oil and fire were everywhere. I searched frantically for a path through it.

"I can't reach you," I called. "Come to me. I'll put out any fire on you."

Across the flames, Cybele spat at me. She spun, heading for a balcony. In doing so, though, the end of her long hair swung through the flames. The entire shining jade mass exploded into deadly, writhing orange.

"*Cybele*." I fought to reach her but the flames seared my throat, driving me back. "CYBELE!"

She screamed only once and that, I swear, not in pain or fear. She shrieked in hate. "*Meddling bastard!*"

Then I was choking on heat and flame and smoke. I stumbled backward out of the room and down the steps. Flame raced along the stair carpeting after me. I did not try to save the tapes or computer in my room. I fled straight for the reception hall and out through the front door into the pelting rain. At the first of the pines lining the driveway, I stopped to cough the smoke out of my lungs. I looked back.

The fire was spreading rapidly. In the seconds I watched, flame skipped along the stairways and blossomed into new brilliance in each room. The heat must have finally activated the generator. Lights came on all over the house. Along with them, holos appeared. For a few bizarre minutes, a dozen Cybeles wandered unconcernedly through the flames. Cleopatra and Anne Boleyn danced up the burning stairs. And then, as Cybele's room blazed high and the stairway tubes twisted and melted, the lights went out again. The Cybeles faltered, flickering, and, one by one, were swallowed by the flames.

Shadow Dance

⦿○○○○○○○○○○○○○○○C○○○○

    Shadow Dance is forever with me. Though I
have never staged it again, its techniques appear in
much that I choreograph these days, and sometimes,
when I am watching a rehearsal in the infrared viewing mode so that the dancers are transformed by the
microelectronics of my eyes from flesh to bright patterns of heat, creatures of light and fire wearing incandescent auras, I am suddenly once more in the
Esrey villa in Aventine, choreographing *Shadow
Dance*.

    Brightest among my glowing troupe is David Barth,
who handles his partner with such tenderness that I
know he sees her as Genea Dane. Then through the
radiant forms comes the cold, dark shadow of Lenore
Esrey, and as my heart contracts in anguish, the present me wishes desperately that I could reach into the
past, to warn David that he dances no golden *pas de
deux* with his partner, real or imagined, but a fatal
pas de trois with love and death.

    In the first lean years after I formed my own
dance troupe, the appearance in Gateside's Blue
Orion Theatre, however brief, came as a rich plum.
We worked hard to demonstrate our talent to stargate
travelers, human and alien, and to the rich, powerful,
and famous who might come over from their hide-
aways in nearby Aventine for an evening's entertainment. We even rehearsed hard, dancing full out
rather than just marking steps, despite a windowless
rehearsal hall and air conditioning that had long since
lost the battle to the heat produced by thirteen exert-
ing bodies.

I danced, too, leading the steps and calling the count. "One, two, three, and one, two, three, four, five."

With the others, between counts I cursed the heat and the sweat. Sweat is a familiar inevitable by-product of dancing, but we were drowning in it. It ran down our foreheads to sting our eyes, darkened our fancifully dyed hair to uniform drab, and soaked the motley assortment of tights, leotards, half-skirts, dance belts, T-shirts, and rubber and knit leg warmers we wore during practice. It dropped onto the floor and, during fast turns, flew off us to spatter others nearby.

"Watch your spacing," I said to Peter Fox. "Three, four, five." And to Susan Jaegar: "You're losing the line, Susan. One, two, three."

We moved into a turn and John Bayonne, slipping on a patch of sweat, fell flat on his back.

I rushed to him. "Are you all right?"

He sat up and wiggled his ankle experimentally. "I think so."

"Take a break, kids," I said. We could not afford injuries, so I wanted to check his ankle myself.

While I knelt beside John, the others headed for dance bags, stacked against the walls under the *barres,* to wipe their faces with towels already soaked by pre-vious wipings, splash on cologne in a valiant try to cool off and smell like something other than livestock, and to gulp down cans of soda, hot and long since flat but still liquid. Their conversation flowed around me, a medley of gossip, complaints about the heat and ach-ing feet, and speculation on the troupe's future.

. I heard the door open but, with my concern about John's ankle, paid little attention until I became aware that the chatter had died away. Then I looked up to catch the newcomers' reflection in the mirrors that stretched the entire length of the wall opposite the door. Bill Ault, the Blue Orion's manager, stood in the doorway with an unfamiliar woman beside him.

I came up off my knees, combing fingers through my sodden hair as I turned. I remembered I had taken off my glasses to dance, and I hurried over to where they hung on the *barre*. Meeting new people, I am very self-conscious about my eyes, which tend to make some people nervous. Only when I felt secure behind the dark lenses did I go to meet Ault and the woman.

In the steaming heat of the rehearsal hall, she looked like a shaft of ice. Taller than any of the dancers in the troupe, taller than I but dancer lean, she wore all white: stiletto-heeled boots, narrow trousers, and a tailored jacket of glistening silk, a thin scarf knotted around her throat. What I could see of her face, framed by a white-blonde helmet of hair and hidden behind oversize sunglasses, looked pale and perfect as sculptured marble—and as stiff—that classic beauty routinely created by a surgeon's scalpel and recreated time and again to keep the woman eternally youthful, but this time unfortunately masklike, as though the man-made face were barely tolerated by the natural bones that wore it.

"Chris," Ault said, "I'd like to have you meet Lenore Esrey. Lenore, this is Christopher Lloyd."

She showed no awareness of the heat or reek of the hall. Expressionless, she extended a hand to me. "Good afternoon, Mr. Lloyd." The hand felt like dry ice, but instead of the matching voice that I would have expected, she sounded like a singer who has sung too much, too loud, in too many smoke-filled bars. "May we talk?"

"Use my office," Ault said.

I glanced around at the kids and pointed at David Barth. "Practice until I come back. Call the count for it, David." Then, draping a towel around my neck, I followed Ault and the woman to the manager's office.

Ault had a window. It looked out over Gateside toward Diana Mountain. The peak rose against a backdrop of cobalt July sky so clear that the buildings near the summit that housed the stargate and put Gateside at the crossroads of the galaxy showed in sharp detail, although compared to their surroundings, they shrank into insignificance. Turning back to Lenore Esrey, I was struck suddenly by her similarity to the frozen, remote beauty of the mountain.

"What did you want to talk to me about?"

"Using your troupe, Christopher. May I call you Christopher?"

Behind the huge glasses, her pale face remained impassive, and I had no idea what to read into words delivered in that incongruous smoke-and-whiskey voice. "Using us for what?" I asked politely.

She sat down, crossing white-sheathed legs. Ault hovered, reaching out to light her cigarette. "I've been a patron of the arts for many years. Once upon a time, I aspired to be a painter. Fortunately, I had the sense to realize my talent was small before I had wasted my life on something that could not be, so I married well instead and now do what I can to help those more gifted than I. I'm one of the people responsible for bringing your troupe to Gateside."

"In fact, bringing you was originally her idea," Ault said.

An angel. No wonder Ault hovered. I sat down, watching her with new interest. "I'm gateful, Mrs. Esrey. Thank you."

"Lenore, please. You're quite welcome. I've been following your career with great interest." While my brows went up, she blew out a thin stream of smoke. "I met a dancer a couple of years ago during a benefit we were organizing. Your name came up. The dancer mentioned having been in classes with you at Juilliard and the Ballet Theatre School, then told me how you went blind later. The story piqued my interest, and I've kept track of you ever since."

Blind. I shuddered at the word. I probably always will, thinking how close I came to it. Without prosthetic eyes, I would now be trapped in a world of endless dark, without dance—functionally dead.

I changed the subject. "What did you mean about using my troupe?"

She tapped the ash from her cigarette. "You've been doing some unusual things, mixing ballet and exotic movements. What would you call yourself, a postmodern neoclassicist?"

I grimaced. "I don't try to label what I do. I just do what seems appropriate or interesting."

Her head tilted to follow the smoke of her cigarette

upward. "One critic calls you a synthesis of Petipa, Balanchine, Twyla Tharp, and Kei Takei."

I raised a brow. She *must* be following me closely. That review had appeared in an obscure avant-garde weekly in San Francisco. But as I recalled, the supposed synthesis had not struck that reviewer as particularly desirable. I said, "I need to go back to rehearsal. Can we please discuss what you want?"

The invisible eyes regarded me for a moment; then she stubbed out her cigarette. "I have a personal project in mind. Have you ever choreographed anything for infrared?"

I stared at her. "Infrared?"

"Yes. You have infrared vision, I know. I realize it was included in your prostheses to augment your night vision, but surely someone as creative as you doesn't limit an ability to just the function the designers intended."

To be honest, I had never even considered using infrared in my work, but I found myself reluctant to admit that to her. "Who would be able to appreciate the pattern except me?" I asked.

She smiled, a faint, stiff tightening of her lips that never disturbed the rest of her face. "Me," she replied in her smoke-and-whiskey voice.

Reaching up, she removed her sunglasses. Shock traveled up my spine as I looked into her eyes. They stared back at me from between lids black outlined in the elaborate Egyptian/Nefertiti style, blind seeming, eyes without pupils whose solid irises glittered gold. She looked blind, but I knew she was not—knew because identical eyes looked back at me from every mirror I faced.

Lenore Esrey folded her glasses and slipped them into her purse. "I could appreciate infrared patterns, Christopher."

With her action, I understood that where I wear dark glasses to hide the oddity of my prostheses, she had done it only for the dramatic effect of this moment, that normally she faced the world without camouflage. Her makeup, colorless except for the elaborate design around her eyes, was obviously intended to emphasize those eyes, to flaunt them.

"I don't patronize only the performing arts. I've just added a new piece of sculpture to my collection, a kinetitrope by Drummond Caspar. Have you heard of him?"

I had to shake my head.

"A fine talent. I intend to show off the sculpture at a party I'm giving in four weeks, and for entertainment I want a dance celebrating it to be performed around the sculpture, aesthetically satisfying whether viewed normally or in infrared."

I stared at her. "A dance for both visual modes simultaneously?" One I knew I could do. Choreography for infrared offered an interesting problem. Making a dance work both ways, though—what a challenge that would be.

The blind-seeming golden eyes looked straight at me. "A difficult demand, perhaps, but I'm willing to pay well for the effort." And she named a figure that would have bought the soul of a far greater mortal than I.

I nodded. She could have had me for the challenge alone, a two-level dance made on a sculpture. "Your party is in four weeks?"

"Yes, so you'll need to begin work as soon as you finish your appearance here." Taking a checkbook from her purse, she began writing. "I'll give you half your money now. Take the cabletrain to Aventine at the end of your engagement. Your whole troupe will be guests at my villa until after your performance. There's plenty of room and a room that will serve for rehearsals." Standing, she handed me the check. "I'll see you in Aventine."

I looked from her departing back to the check in my hand and gripped it hard to reassure myself of its reality.

As though reading my mind, Ault said, "It won't dissolve or bounce. Luther Esrey left her more money than she can possibly spend in her lifetime."

"Left? What happened to him?" I asked.

"It was fifteen years ago—before my time—but the

story I've heard says he was drinking, not an unusual circumstance for him, when somehow the villa caught fire. He was too drunk to save himself. Lenore nearly died, too, going upstairs after her daughter, who was sleeping."

Something in his manner suggested more to the story than he said. "And?" I prompted.

He shrugged uncomfortably. "Nothing, really. There's a bit of gossip that surfaces from time to time. I'm sure rumor is all it is, but—it's been hinted that Lenore started the fire herself."

"What! Why?"

He shrugged again. "They say Luther could be very abusive when he drank heavily. But an investigation didn't find anything, and can you imagine someone starting a fire that would endanger her daughter's life, then almost kill herself rescuing the girl?"

I stared at him. "Was that when she lost her eyes?"

He nodded. "And her face is what the cosmeti-sculpture surgeons were able to restore." He paused. "She knows many people in the theater. Pleasing her almost guarantees good future engagements for your troupe."

That was the news I took back to the kids, along with the check. I had a hard time deciding whether they were more excited by those or by the idea of living in a villa in Aventine for a few weeks. They cavorted around the rehearsal hall in sheer exuberance. David spun down the length of the room in a series of *tours jetés*, then cartwheeled back. I tightened the muscles around my eyes to activate the circuits that added infrared to my vision. In that mode, I still saw the rehearsal hall, but David ceased to look human. He became, instead, a radiant shadow, a being of un-earthly beauty.

The others, too, seemed like members of some ex-otic new species, firebirds, filling the rehearsal hall with their bright glory. Those who were barefoot left a glowing trail behind them on the floor as they moved, and when the dancers touched, their heat patterns flowed together, fusing into a single form.

I noted it all with breathless fascination, wondering

why, in the three years I had had my prostheses, I had never watched dancers this way before and storing my observations against the day I needed them to build dance patterns.

By the end of rehearsal, however, my exhilaration had faded, and doubt began gnawing at me. There was too much light. Soon I could tell nothing about what the kids were doing because they all blended together in a single incandescent fog of heat.

Still in practice clothes, we trooped down the street for tall, icy drinks in the shadowed coolness of the Beta Cygnus Café. The kids capered playfully, hamming for the patrons—David kissed Delia Rose and Kate Massey, then blew one at Frankie Vermilion when the latter archly suggested equal time—before settling down to their cold drinks and gossip. Several announced what they would do with the money they received dancing for Lenore Esrey.

I wondered if we would be able to keep the present check and collect the rest of the fee. Dancing is hot, hard work, as my sweat-soaked practice clothes, clinging cold and clammy to my skin, graphically reminded me. Every time the kids came on stage, they would radiate that same blinding confusion of heat. How could I build a dance of it?

And if pleasing Lenore Esrey meant rewards, what might be the price of displeasing her?

I tried to put it out of my mind, at least until the demands of the Blue Orion appearance were over. I thought I managed to. I caught David glancing curiously at me from time to time, but he said nothing. On the cabletrain for Aventine, however, the barriers broke. Staring out the window, down the hundreds of meters to the mountainsides falling away below, I wondered in earnest how I could make the dance Lenore wanted. It would be like trying to project a light show on the surface of the sun.

Around me, the kids were in high spirits, enjoying every minute of the trip. They made their way up and down the length of the car, clutching at each other in mock fear each time the train swung on its cable, chatting and flirting with other passengers. As healthy, attractive young people, they found ready response. Two particularly stunning young women became the object of Gerry Petrie and Phil Burby's attention, but while they reciprocated, their eyes, I noticed, kept slipping toward David. He, on the other hand, appeared totally unaware of them, involved instead in a conversation with a middle-aged woman whose raw, angular bones looked grossly clumsy next to David's slim good looks.

His choice of the woman over the girls did not surprise me. I had noticed before how David seemed to gravitate toward lame ducks. I *was* surprised, though, to look up at the sound of my name a short while later and find him standing beside me.

"You left your friend?" I asked.

"I saw you from back there. I thought maybe it might help if you could talk about what's bothering you."

So my anxiety showed, after all. His concern warmed me, though for a moment it made me feel as if I were the younger of us instead of nearly ten years his senior. Then the moment passed, and with it, the urge to confide in him. Why burden a boy with my worries? I tapped my head. "I'm working. Sometimes creativity is a painful process."

He looked dubious. "You're sure that's all it is?"

I made myself smile. "We'll work it out in rehearsal."

That appeared to satisfy him, and he moved away down the car, toward the stunning girls this time, though pausing on the way to blow a kiss at a pudding-plump teen-ager who watched the dancers with wistful envy. Even in normal vision, I noticed, David seemed glazed with golden light. Then I returned to worrying about infrared choreography.

I was still worrying when the two white limousines that met us at the cabletrain deposited us on the steps of the Esrey villa. Lenore met us there. Wearing white again—boots, slacks, and a blouse that buttoned high at the neck and tight at the wrists—the sun shining on her ice-pale hair, she resembled the statues lining the drive. As she came down the steps, a mountain breeze curled around me, as though coming from Lenore herself, cool but subtly edged in ice, sending a shiver through me even in the midsummer sun. The light had darkened the photosensitive covering of her eyes to near black, so that instead of gold eyes, I faced obsidian marbles.

She nodded to us. "Welcome to Aventine. The servants will take your luggage. Let me show you around."

We followed her inside to where a broad staircase swept upward around the edge of a cavernous hall.

"For the purpose of the party, the sculpture will be in here," Lenore said. "You'll perform around it."

The kids' wide-eyed stares vanished as they began a professional study of what would be our stage. I was pleased to see that instead of terrazo or tile, the floor was parquet. I took a step and leaped experimentally. The wood had good spring. I slipped and nearly fell on landing, though, and knelt to run fingers across the surface.

"Do you suppose you could have some of the wax removed before the performance?" I asked.

Lenore nodded. "Whatever you need. If you'll come this way, I'll show you the rehearsal area."

She led us through doors at the far end of the hall onto a terrace. Below it lay a pool area. The kids poked each other in delight.

"May we use the pool?" Kate Massey asked.

"You're guests," Lenore replied. "Feel free to use any of the villa's facilities. You might be interested in the Heliomere, too. The steps down to the water are over there." She pointed toward a ballustrade visible where the lawn ended in a cliff overlooking the lake. "Thermal springs keep it about thirty-five degrees."

David grinned. "A lake-sized bath. My muscles will love soaking in——" He broke off, staring past me.

I turned to follow his line of sight and found myself almost face to face with a young woman in a beach wrap. I did not blame David for staring. The girl coming out of the villa was lovely, with warm brown eyes, a long, silky mane of copper hair, and a golden tan that gave her the look of light shining out of her.

Seeing us, the girl started to retreat across the terrace but stopped at the sound of Lenore's voice.

"Genea, I thought you were resting."

"I wanted to—soak in the Heliomere a bit." The girl's voice came light as the fine, birdlike bones visible under her skin. Her eyes swept our group, and she gave us a shy smile. "Are you the dancers?"

A slight depression appeared in the skin between Lenore's eyebrows. "You know I don't like having you down there alone. Find one of the servants to go with you."

"But I'll be perfectly all—" Lenore said nothing, just looked at the girl, but the girl broke off and turned back toward the house.

David's were not the only pair of male eyes that followed her, but his lingered longest on the doorway where she disappeared.

"A beautiful girl," I said.

Lenore's obsidian Nefertiti eyes turned on me. "My daughter."

I remembered then that Bill Ault had mentioned one, but I found it hard to accept that this sunshine creature sprang from the cold marble of Lenore.

We followed Lenore to a far wing of the villa, into a large sunny room with a bank of windows looking across the Heliomere, one mirrored wall, and portable *barres* standing along the other three on heavy cast-iron legs and feet. The floor was tiled, but a test jump told me good wood lay beneath, and the wax on the tile had been neglected enough to make acceptable footing.

"Did you dance, too?" I asked.

"No. I had it cleared and the *barres* brought in for you. It was an exercise room for my son-in-law." The smoke-and-whiskey voice carried an undertone of distaste.

Looking, I could see perceptibly lighter areas on the tile where exercise equipment had once stood.

"Will this suit you? Is there anything I can add?" Lenore asked. "A piano, perhaps? A tape player?"

"I have a tape player." I carried it everywhere, with the tapes of our music. So often we performed where an orchestra was an unheard-of extravagance, and I had had terrible experiences trying to teach even a pianist the proper tempi overnight. "This looks fine."

She went on to show us the rest of the villa. I saw sculpture and paintings everywhere but had no time to look closely at them as we passed. I decided I would come back and study them later. Perhaps they would tell me something of the woman who owned them and suggest what might please her in a dance.

We came finally to a long room filled with sculpture and paintings, obviously her formal gallery. Lenore led us to a tall, shrouded shape at the end and with a flourish whipped off the muffling cover.

"This is the Caspar sculpture," she said. *"Pillar of Cloud."*

It stood three meters on its base, a slender, irregular column of a frothy-textured tropic material. As Lenore moved around it, a slow ripple traveled up its length, altering the convexities and concavities.

"Pillar of Cloud," I said. The title reminded me of Antony Tudor's ballet *Pillar of Fire*.

Lenore's lips performed their stiff parody of a smile. "Are you thinking of the Tudor ballet? I did, too. That's why I decided dancers should celebrate its acquisition. It's fitting, too, because this is a kinetitrope."

Pillar of Fire would have been a more fitting title for a dance choreographed for infrared, I reflected, then began studying the sculpture to see if its nature suggested a dance. The kids surrounded it. They moved near, and it responded in the slow way of tropes, bulging toward them as if asking to be touched. Watching, I began to see a dance in my mind. This sculpture called for something ethereal and floating, something balletic. *Pillar of Cloud* would be the center, with the line and steps focusing on it, drawing the audience's eyes to it. I saw no trouble staging a dance for ordinary viewing, but—how could I make it work in infrared as well?

I tightened my facial muscles to add on the infrared capability and watched the kids that way. *Pillar of Cloud* rose cool and dark amid the warm shapes. I could see each member of the troupe distinctly now, even identify them. Their body heat was not so great that it obscured the details visible to my underlying normal vision. But that was only because they were at rest, so to speak. The moment they warmed up to dance, that would change.

I realized belatedly that Lenore had been trying to talk to me for several moments. I turned toward her, blinking. Even in infrared, she looked cooler than the rest of us. I switched back to ordinary vision and met her eyes, blind-looking gold once more. "I'm sorry. What did you say?"

"I asked if you wanted to see your rooms now or after lunch."

After lunch would be fine, I decided. We would be wanting to change into practice clothes then.

Lunch, served in a large formal dining room with Lenore at one end of the long table, was simple and light, food that would digest easily. Lenore ate with us, but no other members of the household did.

"Your daughter and her husband aren't having lunch?" I asked.

The gold eyes stared somewhere past me. "My daughter is no longer married," was all she replied, and turned away to chat with Meg Wolfe and Thea Keach on the other side of the table from me.

In the afternoon, we put on practice clothes, and I held a ballet class. We started at the *barre,* warming up with *pliés* and *battements tendus.*

"I think I know what this dance is going to be," Jae Ann Isley said. "Will we be on *pointe?*"

"I've no intention of being *that* traditional," I said. "Come on, Thea, *stretch* your leg. Straighten your back, Peter. One and two and three."

Twelve legs snapped out, reaching in turn to the floor in front, the side, and then the rear, backs erect, faces intent with eyes turned inward in concentration or fastened on the images in the mirror.

Later, joining them at the center work in the middle

of the room, I watched our mirror images in the infrared mode and saw with a feeling of frustration that
the heat we radiated blurred our images to the point I
could not tell who was who or exactly what they were
doing with their bodies. Remembering how I had
thought of them as firebirds the day I first looked at
them this way, I wondered if perhaps the answer was
to have them dance as flamelike characters, weaving
in and out of each other around the sculpture. That
struck no tone of *rightness* in me, however. It seemed
flat, uninteresting.

I sighed. There must be a way to use this peculiarity
of Lenore's and my eyes to create something unique,
something that had never been done before and could
not be realized except through our kind of vision. For
the moment, though, I had no idea what that might
be or how to do it.

After ninety minutes of class, we were soaked with
sweat, despite faithful air conditioning, and ready for a
break. A maid appeared with icy glasses of tea and
lemonade, and I was glad I had thought to arrange
it. We drank them gratefully, sitting sprawled on the
floor, massaging aching muscles that had not been
used for that much ballet since we began our tour.

A face peered in through a window. I recognized
Lenore's daughter and beckoned to her. She hesitated
but after a few minutes came to the door from the terrace and with a quick look back over her shoulder,
stepped in. She stood clutching her beach wrap around
her and looking at the room.

"It's bigger without Giles' things in it." Then her
eyes came down to me. "I'm Genea Dane. You must
be Christopher Lloyd; you have eyes like mother's."

"Join us?" I gestured to the tray of drinks.

She refused a drink but sat down cross-legged on
the floor with us. "I'm so happy to have you here.
This house is such a barn with the two of us rattling
around in it." She smiled around. "Who are you all?"

I hastily introduced the troupe. She acknowledged
each name with a nod. "It's nice to meet you. You
looked just beautiful dancing. Was what I saw part of
the dance you'll do at the party?"

"I haven't started working on that yet," I said.

"Oh." The word carried disappointment. "When will you?"

"Just as soon as we've rested a bit."

She toyed with the hem of her robe. "Would you mind if I watched?"

I never object to anyone watching class or to spectators in later rehearsals, but in the early stages of choreography, when I am experimenting, seeing which combinations seem to fit and which fail, outsiders distract me; make me feel self-conscious. I was saved the unpleasantness of refusing Genea's request, though.

She stiffened, listening for a moment, then jumped up. "I think I hear my mother coming. I have to go. Please, you won't tell her I was here, will you?" She fled through the door from the terrace.

David looked after her with concern in his eyes.

Moments later, Lenore came in through the hall door. She did not stay long, just asked if we found everything all right and with a quick glance around, left again. I wondered if she had been looking for Genea.

I accomplished little toward the dance that afternoon. We set the tray of glasses in the center of the floor to represent the sculpture, and I let the kids ad lib steps around it. I found several combinations I would have used if the dance had been limited to normal vision, but in infrared they came across as only a confusion of light. With a sigh, I gave it up for the day. We changed to swim suits and submerged our aches in the soothing heat of the Heliomere. Soaking, I had time to wonder about Lenore and Genea, the latter's fear of her mother, and Lenore's seemingly reluctance to let her daughter meet us. I wondered if the girl would be at dinner.

She came, and Lenore introduced her—as Genea *Esrey,* however, not *Dane* as Genea had done that afternoon—but Genea remained close to her mother the entire meal, eyes downcast, saying hardly a word. It was the same on several succeeding nights. She did peep at us from time to time, and each time found David looking at her, so by the fourth evening, she was deliberately seeking his eyes. When she found them, she gave him a quick, shy smile before looking away again. Either Lenore did not mind the distant flirtation, or she failed to notice it, but when David tried to speak to Genea, to say something beyond a casual amenity, Lenore moved between them and took the girl down the room with her.

The cut was so blunt I decided to find out what she had against us. After Genea had gone upstairs for the evening, I asked to speak to Lenore in the library.

"Is there something you need?" she asked when we were alone.

"I want to talk about Genea."

I would not have thought it possible for her face to freeze, but somehow it did. "My daughter is none of your concern, Christopher. You're here to choreograph a dance. How is it coming, by the way?"

I refused to be sidetracked. "Genea *is* my concern. Perhaps I should be flattered—people don't generally feel the need to lock up their *daughters* around dancers—but your attitude has given my troupe the feeling they must have something disgusting and contagious. What is it you think we're going to do to Genea?"

The blind-gold eyes glittered coldly. "Genea is very vulnerable. She's recovering from a disastrous marriage to a man whose only real interest in her was proving his irresistible charm by convincing her to elope with him and using her money—*my* money—to finance his grand prix race cars. I intend to see that no one ever harms her like that again. Now that I've told you, I expect you to assume responsibility for your people's conduct. Any sign of what I consider reprehensible behavior will instantly terminate your employment here. Do I make myself clear?"

She did. Breathing hard and feeling myself for mortal wounds, I escaped from the library. Instead of going back to the others, though, I chose the terrace and sat on the parapet, letting the night breeze cool me. Overhead, stars glittered brilliantly through the mountain air, mirroring the lights of Aventine shining across the Heliomere and on down the mountain side.

Only gradually did I become aware of whispers in the darkness somewhere near me. I switched my vision to infrared and looked for the source. Finally, I spotted two warm shapes through the open door of the pool cabana. One of the two laughed, and I recognized the voice instantly: David's. Who was he out here with, though? The height of the second form, taller than David's, ruled out any of the girls or boys in the troupe. One of the maids, perhaps? Then, with a sudden chill, I suspected who it was. Carefully, soundlessly, I made my way around the pool to be sure.

Stepping into the doorway of the cabana, I said, "Hello, Genea."

She started but recovered well. "David and I were just—"

I cut her off. "Why with the door open?"

"So we could see anyone coming," David said.

"You didn't see me, but with infrared I saw you very clearly from the terrace."

They moved uneasily, not missing the significance of that.

"I'd whisper a bit more softly, too, if I were you," I added. I left them, closing the door behind me.

After I was in bed, David came to my room. "Thank you for warning us and closing the door."

I sat up in bed and looked at him sitting on the edge, warm in the darkness. "You could have gotten us fired." I repeated to him what Lenore had told me.

David said earnestly, "We weren't doing anything wrong, just talking. I'm not playing with her."

I believed him. David would not, not like Phil Burby or Gerry Petrie, who both had a long series of conquests and one-night stands. The question, of course, was would Lenore believe him? "You'd be safer talking in broad daylight, in the open, where Lenore can *see* nothing is happening."

"But she won't let Genea talk at all. Chris, the girl is lonely and desperately unsure of herself. Her mother has always run her life, told her everything to do. Marrying Giles Dane was the one independent act of her life, and that turned out to be a mistake. She needs to be convinced that she's still capable of making decisions and running her own life."

I sighed. Lame-duck time again. At least this one was pretty. "Be careful, then."

He nodded.

In the morning, taking the time I had promised myself to look at the paintings in the upper hall, I found a portrait of Genea. The girl looked more self-assured than the one I knew, suggesting it had been done early in her marriage, but the coloring was the same: golden-tan skin, warm brown eyes, and a wealth of copper hair piled formally on her head for the sitting. Studying the image, I found it more incredible than ever that Genea and Lenore could be daughter and mother. I could hardly imagine two more opposite people—like sun and moon, fire and ice. They might grow more alike in time, though, as night and cold smothered sunlight. I hoped David could find a way to heal his lame duck before that could happen.

The other paintings in the hallway all appeared to have mythical subjects, but with oddly familiar faces, particularly one in ancient Greek armor with a background of a walled city and great wooden horse. I frowned at the face for some time, trying to place it, before I gave up and moved on.

The paintings, obviously by the same artist, had been executed with what even I recognized as fair technical skill, but they lacked the life and vitality I saw in other paintings around the house. Heroes, centaurs, fauns, and gods looked out of these canvases at me with frozen faces like death masks. What had moved Lenore to buy so many works from the same poor artist?

Then I saw the signature at the bottom of each: L. For Lenore, perhaps? In Ault's office, she had mentioned having painted at one time. If these paintings were hers, it would explain their presence among the superior work scattered through the rest of the villa. I looked at the dates next to each signature. All fell within the last fifteen years. It would seem that she still painted a little.

I stood back and looked over the group as a whole. She liked mythical subjects. Costumes of a Greek style might appeal to her, then. Should I use a mythological theme in the dance, too?

I carried that possibility with me through class and the morning rehearsal session, but nothing came of it. I ran both hands through my sweat-damp hair. Almost a week gone and still no firm idea of the dance. I could feel panic starting to chew at me. Lenore and Genea had gone down to Aventine's shopping square, so I was saved facing our patron at lunch, but she walked right into the middle of afternoon rehearsal. Without warning, the hall door opened, and Lenore appeared, a narrow, dark shadow contrasting sharply with the bright ones of the dancers.

"I thought I would see how you're doing," she said.

If only I could use her in the dance, I mused. Playing her darkness against the dancers would make a pattern and provide interest. Then my breath quickened. Contrast, I thought.

"Could I see some of the dance, Christopher?" the smoke-and-whiskey voice asked.

Something was happening in the back of my head. I could not see it yet, could not touch it, but I felt it— a deep scrambling of thought, a soundless closing of switches. For the first time, I felt hope.

I said, "Wouldn't you rather wait until the party and see the entire dance, in its proper place and costumes?"

Her eyes showed in infrared as black, heatless holes. "I would like to approve the dance before it's presented to my guests. A number of art critics, several of them also familiar with dance, will be attending. You can understand I want them to be impressed with both the sculpture and its presentation."

Behind her, I noticed a second shadow. She had allowed Genea to come with her. While Lenore talked, the second shadow edged sideways toward the radiant form of David Barth.

I shifted position, so that to keep her eyes on me, Lenore had to turn her back on David. "I plan at least one dress rehearsal. Anyone who wants can see it then, and you may come to rehearsals the last week, too, if you wish. Right now, there really isn't much to see but disconnected combinations."

She appeared to believe the lie. She nodded. "Very well."

She turned to find Genea and leave. To give the girl and David a few more minutes, I said hurriedly, "I've been thinking about costumes. I'd like to discuss them with you."

"As you wish."

"Let's talk on the terrace and get out of the way. You're on your own for a few minutes, kids."

We moved outside. I talked costumes, tossing out any idea that occurred to me but not listening to what I said. Through the window, I could see the kids, some resting, some working at the *barre* to stay warmed up, a few couples practicing lifts and catches. And I could see David, standing motionless talking to Genea. As he cooled off, his body color dimmed. I noted the range of heat between Genea and Lenore, the kids cooling down, and those still working. The observation dropped into the elusive churning in the back of my head, where it rang with the purity of a crystal bell. *That* was what I needed for the dance, but—how could I use it? A dancer who danced without warming up could not perform at optimum and, worse, invited injury. Still there must be a way to produce a pattern with a range of body heats.

I felt another soundless click in my head. A memory surfaced but floated just out of reach. I strained for it. I had seen or heard something—something in a ballet. I cursed silently. I knew I had what I needed to know, but the damned thing persisted in eluding me.

"The ideas all sound good," Lenore said. "You'll need to decide definitely within a few days, though, if they're to be made in time." She started to turn away again.

I stopped her again, this time for myself rather than Genea and David. Out here, I felt close to the answer I needed. If I went back inside, I was afraid it would sink out of sight again. "Are those your paintings in the upper hall?"

Her arrested movement indicated surprise. "Yes." Her voice hesitated. "Some fanciful portraits of friends for my own amusement."

Friends? They had all been male. I wondered briefly if they had been lovers, placed in the hallway so that she could see them every day as she went to and from her bedroom.

"Some of the faces look familiar."

"They are all well known for one reason or another. Tell me, what do you think of my work?"

I should have been expecting that. I hunted for a good evasion. "I'm no judge of painting."

"Perhaps sculpture interests you more, being a sculpture of sorts yourself?"

I blinked in surprise. "I beg your pardon?"

The lightless eyes watched me. "Don't you sculpt in bodies and sound? Given that you're no art critic, you must still have a personal opinion of the paintings, though. What is it?"

I saw no way out. What to say, then? She had given up being an artist because she realized she lacked enough talent, so surely she would recognize a flattering lie. Did she want one, anyway, or would she resent it?

On impulse, I tried honesty. "I think you were wise to choose buying art over creating it."

She stared at me a moment, then laughed, a brittle sound of cool amusement. "You are extraordinary, Christopher—a man of truth. Well, on that note, I'll let you return to work—and trust that you'll have more to show at the performance than ballet exercises. Genea! Come along."

I flushed. So she was quite well aware how poorly the dance was progressing.

Then her words clanged against the elusive memory —a performance with ballet exercises. *Etudes!* That was the ballet I needed to remember—the key. Dazzled with relief and inspiration, I stared after the cold mistress of the villa. *That* was how to do the dance!

I charged back into our rehearsal hall and clapped

my hands for attention. They came alert, sensing the change in me. "We have our dance, kids." I divided them into three groups of four and explained what we were going to do.

Frankie Vermilion frowned. "Come on stage *cold?* Chris, you know my hamstrings. I can't dance a step before I warm up."

"You'll have your warmup," I promised.

Then we began work in earnest.

The days fell into a regular pattern, class and a short rehearsal in the morning, a long rehearsal in the afternoon. The dance gradually took shape. A swim in the Heliomere followed rehearsal to soak away the aches and pains of dancing. Because we rarely saw anyone but each other in the water, we took to swimming without suits and acquired all-over tans. In the evening, we played in the game room or watched television or some of the holotape dramas and symphonies in Lenore's collection. Sometimes we improvised dances to the symphonies, creating uncanny effects by dancing through the performers and settings in the holographic projections.

I tried to occupy Lenore's attention as much as possible, to keep her from playing watchdog over Genea, so the girl could have time with David. They looked beautiful together, two golden young people who glowed around each other.

Ordinarily, Lenore could not have helped but see what was happening, but the entire troupe became conspirators against her. As if by accident, they always stood between Lenore and Genea, blocking the older woman's vision, and when Genea came to practice, everyone watched for Lenore. If she happened by the rehearsal room, they would bunch in a group around Genea until Lenore left again.

Occupying Lenore turned out to be a less unpleasant task than I anticipated, though. I never felt really at ease with her, but listening to her could be fascinating. As Luther Esrey's wife, and later as his widow, she had met many interesting and important people. She talked about them with complete candor. I have sometimes wondered since what might have happened between us if she had been younger, closer to my own age, and my height or smaller instead of requiring me always to look up at her. I sometimes shudder, wondering.

I suspected Genea and David saw each other alone after Genea had ostensibly gone to bed, but I did not learn they had started sleeping together until three days before our performance. John Bayonne tapped on my door one night and asked if he could sleep on the couch in my room.

"What's wrong with your bed?" I asked.

John grinned. "David has me locked out. Three's a crowd."

I felt my newly acquired tan disappear in one split second of horror. That boy had gone raving mad! If Lenore caught them—

I headed for David's room and pounded on the door. "It's Chris. I want to talk to you."

His voice came through from the other side. "Can you come back later? I'm—"

"You've lost your mind is what you've done," I hissed. "You're the best dancer I have, David, me boy, but I'm not about to lose this job for anyone." I lowered my voice still more and hissed through the keyhole, "Get her *out of there!*"

After a moment, he replied softly, "All right."

I started back for my room, only to stop short at the sight of Lenore coming up the hallway. I whirled to study the nearest painting. As she came nearer, I pretended I had just noticed her. "Good evening, Lenore. You're up late, too?"

"I thought I would just look in on Genea before going to bed."

My heart and stomach tangled up. In what I fervently hoped was a casual voice, I asked, "Will you do me a favor first? You said these paintings are all of well-known men. I know this face is familiar, but I've wracked my brain and can't put a name to it." Only then did I realize I was looking at the painting with the Siege of Troy background. "Who is it?"

"Achilles, as portrayed by Senator William Jaspar Johnson."

So that was why I knew his face. His expulsion from the senate in the Sanderman Bribery scandal had put his face on every magazine cover and news program for months. I wondered what to say. Was there a polite comment to make on learning that someone's former lover was a major political villain? "Were you shocked to learn about him?"

Her blind-gold eyes glittered. "Oh, no. I knew all about it. He told me in the course of our relationship."

That made three people who knew about the senator's well-covered tracks, then—the senator, Lenore, and the anonymous person who gave his name to the FBI. "Did he ever tell you who he suspected of informing on him?"

"I never saw him again after the scandal broke. He wouldn't let me. He said it was best in order to protect me. Can you guess who any of the rest are?"

We walked down the hall, with Lenore naming the model of each painting. I recognized another politician, a diplomat, three corporate heads, a couple of actors and military leaders, and one symphonic conductor. I looked at Bacchus wearing the face of Hans Taggart and remembered that he had been fired from the Boston Philharmonic the previous year for drunkenness. Some of the other names I also recognized as connected with dishonoring publicity. This house must have heard a great many secrets over the years.

"A number of your friends have had their share of problems, haven't they?"

I regretted the tactless comment as soon as it was out, but Lenore appeared not to mind. "They were powerful men, and power often carries madness and the seeds of destruction in it. It's what makes such men exciting. I'm fortunate that I knew them during the height of their glory."

That brought the first real expression I had ever seen on her face, a flush of color that turned the glittering gold of her eyes to brass. She ran her tongue over her lips, a quick, darting movement—predatory.

A moment later, the color had gone, and her face was again cool and still as marble.

I fought a sudden desire to run for the safety of my bed. No matter how much I wanted to, I could not leave until I was sure David had returned Genea to her room. "Why did you paint them as mythical subjects?" I asked.

The pale lips stretched in a stiff smile. "It seemed appropriate. Do you know how I see you, for example?"

I shook my head.

"As Lucifer," she said. The smoke-and-whiskey voice almost crooned.

"Lucifer!" I said, startled.

"In the true translation—the Morning Star, the Lord of Light. That's what you look like by infrared." She brought the blind-gold eyes looking down into mine. "It's a shame there's so little time until you perform, no time to sit for me."

No time to become a fallen angel with a death-mask face. "I'm not quite the same class as your other models, anyway."

She moved closer. "You're something better. We share a similar gift of sight, you and I, Christopher. It's going to take you to great heights. I can help see to that."

I believed her, and that tempted and frightened me. Did she know the price of all men so well?

She moved still closer, the blind-gold eyes fixed on mine. Cool air touched me, like cold off ice. I felt helpless to move, unable to breathe, as though I were listening to a Siren or facing the fatal eyes of Medusa.

"Christopher . . ." she began softly.

Then, beyond her down the hallway, someone appeared. "Good evening, mother."

Lenore backed away from me. "Are you still awake?"

"I don't seem to be able to sleep tonight. I was just going down to the kitchen for some milk." Genea carried heat in her cheeks, I saw by infrared, and trailed a tantalizing scent of sweat and musk perfume as she passed us, but her voice and expression betrayed nothing of where she had been. She looked as calmly confident as she appeared in her portrait. David, I reflected, seemed to have been right about her. "Would you like some, too, mother?" she asked.

After glancing at me a moment, Lenore followed her.

"Good night, Christopher," Genea said sweetly.

"A very good night to you, Genea," I replied, and fled for my room.

I thanked the dawn that brought the day of Lenore's party and our performance. By midnight, we would be leaving. I had driven the kids hard the previous few days and avoided Lenore whenever possible. I hardly knew what to call the incident in the hallway—a temptation, perhaps. But I knew I did not want to experience it again.

I intended to say nothing to David, but the following morning he came to me. "I'm in love with Genea," he said.

I was not surprised.

"I'm going to take her with us when we leave."

That made me sigh. Eloping appeared to be her favorite method of leaving home, but I could not blame her for wanting to go or condemn David for planning to take her. The sight of those death masks I had to pass in the upper hallway every day spurred my own desire to leave.

We held a dress rehearsal in the morning. Workmen had moved *Pillar of Cloud* into the great hall and set up a *barre* around it like a protective railing. The kids looked great in their costumes, tank-topped body suits for the boys, fitting like skin, tights and short-skirted dance practice costumes for the girls. The color combinations gave me two couples in red, two in yellow, and two in blue, with hair dyed to match.

Lenore and Genea watched the dress rehearsal. After searching through the troupe's regular music and an assortment of contemporary and classical tapes in Lenore's library, I had finally settled on Ravel's *Bolero,* slightly shortened, to accompany the dance, mostly because of the constant repetition of theme

and mounting intensity. The music was for the benefit of the spectators. Dancing by counts, as they had
learned the choreography, the kids scarcely listened to
their accompaniment.

I realized the choice of music had been wise,
though, when I saw Lenore swaying slightly in time to
it and leaning farther and farther toward the dancers.
I watched her in normal vision between following the
kids in normal and infrared and wished her face
showed expression. At the end, I had to ask how she
liked it.

"I think that even my most discriminating guests
will approve. Do you have a title for it? *Pillar of
Cloud*, perhaps?"

I hate questions for answers. "I call it *Shadow
Dance*. What about your opinion? What do you think
of the dance in infrared?"

The gold-blind eyes looked into mine. "I decided
not to watch it in infrared until this evening. I want
to be surprised. I think I can guess enough of what
you're doing to feel confident I won't be disappointed.
Now, come along, Genea. We have matters to attend
to."

Genea followed her mother, but as she left, she
blew a kiss to David and mouthed at me: *I love it.*

Two servants threw a muffling sheet over the sculpture and the undulations caused by the dance faded,
leaving the trope quiescent. The kids went to change
and take a quick, cooling swim.

The first guests began arriving after lunch. By later
afternoon, the villa overflowed. People wandered
everywhere in the house and on the grounds. Unbro-
ken streams flowed up and down the stairs and
through the dining room where a huge buffet drew
people all day. Rented servants threaded their way
through the crowd with trays of drinks, and a bar
stood open in the game room for those wishing exotic
concoctions.

When I caught glimpses of myself in mirrors, my
eyes were invisible behind my dark glasses, but I suspected they must be as wide as the kids'. None of us
had seen a crowd like this before except at premieres

and opening nights. Among the many people we did
not know, we were able, with some awe, to identify
national and international public figures, multimillion-
aires, actors and other performers, and famous art collectors and critics. We even saw a few people who had
been principals or stars in shows and night clubs we
danced in at one time or another.

One, however—Dale Flood—remembered me, too,
from a telethon we had appeared on the year before.
He pumped my hand enthusiastically, his broad, country face beaming. "How ya doing, Chris?" he boomed
in the famous gravel voice that gave his songs their
distinctive sound. "Lenore always puts on a good
bash, don't ya think?"

"You know her well?" I asked.

"Since Luther married her. Luther and I knocked
around the country together back in the old days
when the two of us had but two shirts, two pairs of
jeans, and a dollar between us." He looked around
the cavernous hall. "This is a hell of a long way from
that. You one of her latest protégés?"

"We're part of the ceremonies."

"Part of the big surprise, huh? Well, I think I'll go
say howdy to the lady."

He grabbed another drink from a passing tray and
headed to where Lenore, with Genea right behind,
was coming down the stairs. Lenore wore a white
body suit that hugged her from neck to wrists and ankles and flashed with occasional icy glitters as she
moved. The blind-gold eyes glittered, too, between the
black-lined lids. In contrast, Genea wore something
soft and of a blue that flattered her coppery warm
color.

I saw David watching for an opportunity to speak
to the girl, but Lenore kept her so close the lovers
could not even have whispered without being heard.

"How am I going to get her away?" David asked in
something like despair.

I gave him a reassuring smile. "Don't worry. We'll
find a way."

I went to make sure that the orchestra, which had
begun setting up in the hall overlook area beyond the

head of the stairs, had the *Bolero* music and knew where to cut it. The director and I discussed tempo. When I felt sure he understood, I glanced at my watch to check the time and sent the kids off to dress in their dance costumes. After that, I could only wait nervously for Lenore to begin her little ceremony.

Finally, at seven o'clock sharp, at a signal from Lemore, the orchestra played a flourish. Servants gently urged guests away from the muffled sculpture until a space was cleared to the proper dimensions. Another servant carried a chair up to the rail around the sculpture and helped Lenore on to it. Silence fell in the crowded hall. I do not remember exactly what Lenore said, something that welcomed everyone and promised them the surprise she had hinted at in her invitations. I heard with only one ear, listening principally for the cue to begin the dance. After dressing, the kids had gone down the back stairs through the kitchen and were waiting inside the dining room for the music.

Then Lenore reached out and with the same flourish she had used the day she first showed the sculpture to us, unveiled *Pillar of Cloud*. The applause and movement of the guests sent a ripple up the length of the kinetitrope. That was our cue. I nodded at the conductor.

David, Jae Ann, Peter, and Meg, wearing yellow, filed out into the clear space as Lenore and the chair left the area. In time to the music, they moved to the trope and reached out for the *barre* around it: one on each side, girl opposite girl, boy opposite boy, moving in unison, their knees bent in warmup *pliés*.

I switched to infrared vision. They showed dimly, as merely normal warm. In the process of stretching and bending, loosening their muscles and joints, their color brightened.

They moved away from the *barre* to become two couples, David and Jae Ann, Peter and Meg, and began partnering exercises.

Now another four filed on, in red, and took their places at the *barre*. The cool of their bodies contrasted to the brighter ones of the first four, and when they began to brighten, the last four came on, wearing blue.

The three temperature levels wove in and out among each other, sometimes disappearing from sight behind the dark shadow of the trope. In response to their motion, the trope quivered and undulated, its surface rolling slowly, suggestive of its namesake.

The intensity of the music climbed. With it, the dancers worked through ever more difficult combinations, lifts, and catches, brightening steadily until their separate identities became lost in the brilliance. As the music reached its climax, they spun, leaped, and returned to the *barre* to grasp it and sink to their knees as though in obeisance to the trope, light paying homage to dark, fire worshipping ice.

And even before I thought how well the kids had done, I thought: *That ought to stroke Lenore's vanity.*

Applause echoed like thunder in the hall, and the trope writhed as the crowd closed murmuring on it, Lenore, and the kids.

Lenore forced her way through the congratulatory guests to me. Her eyes glittered red-gold, reflecting the high color in her face. "Well done, Christopher," she said. "You've earned this." And she handed over a check.

I put it safely inside my jacket.

"Why don't you stay another few days and relax?" she went on. "I would so like to do that painting of you."

I let her well-wishers push between us before I could answer. I backed off through them, looking for the kids. We were finished. We could leave. Relief washed through me, spoiled only by the annoyance at seeing Lenore receiving all the compliments on the sculpture and dance, as though *she* were responsible for them.

One by one, I located the kids and pushed them toward the stairs. "Change and pack. We're leaving."

The crowd had managed to separate Genea from Lenore, too. I pointed that out to David. "Collect her. We'll get out while Lenore is busy, before she has a chance to miss us."

David worked his way toward Genea.

I reached the edge of the worst crush and headed for

the stairs, only to be stopped by Dale Flood. He slapped my shoulder. "Good work. I don't have eyes like yours and Lenore's, but from the way she's looking, you did something very well for her. If no one else here gives you the credit you deserve, I do."

I thanked him.

David and Genea came out of the crowd and passed us, heading up the stairs. Flood looked after them. "She's looking happy tonight. Guess she's over Dane. Not that I expected her to grieve for long." He cocked a brow at me. "Between you and me, I think that marriage would have ended in a divorce if he hadn't died first."

I blinked in surprise. "But I thought—from what Lenore said, I thought they had divorced."

Flood shook his head. "Dane was killed in Monte Carlo about six months ago. It was his own damn fault, too, so I hear. For all the things he wasn't, he was still a fine driver, but he had no business racing when he and Genea had been fighting that way. Those turns take full concentration. Going out mad, he was just asking to crash. Well." He sighed, looking up at David and Genea, stopped at the top of the stairs. "Maybe she'll have better luck next time. She sure is a real beauty, the image of her mother."

Flood never seemed to run out of surprising statements. I stared at him. "The image of her mother? I don't think I've seen two more opposite women." I wished David would take Genea down the hall. Lenore was bound to see them if they remained where they were.

"Not Lenore the way she looks now. Lenore the way she looked before Luther died and her hair went white after the fire. There's a portrait of her up there in the hall done the year Luther married her."

My breath caught in the middle of my chest. The portrait was of *Lenore?*

"You look at that portrait. Lenore and Genea are alike as two peas in a pod," Flood said.

David and Genea started down the hall, but it was too late. I heard Lenore's voice call Genea's name; then Lenore hurried by me up the stairs. I followed.

"Where are you going?" Lenore demanded as we reached the girl and David.

Genea lifted her chin. "I'm leaving with David, mother."

"Don't be ridiculous," Lenore said. "Haven't you had enough of eloping with beautiful young men?"

The chin lifted a fraction more, but it trembled. "It's different this time."

"Really? Can you take care of her, David?" A lash of contempt flicked at him. "What does a dancer earn, even a well-paid one? What are you earning in the Lloyd Troupe?"

Genea's chin came down as she started to wilt. David caught her arm. "Don't let her run your life anymore, Genea. You're your own person. It doesn't matter that you made one mistake. Everyone makes mistakes. It only matters that you learn from them. You're free to go where you want and marry whomever you wish."

Genea froze. Her head snapped toward him. "Marry? I have no intention of marrying again. Mother's right; I *have* had enough of *that*."

David blinked as though stung. "But we talked about—"

"That's all it was, wasn't it?" Genea spread her hands, shrugging helplessly. "How can I marry again? If it doesn't work, there's no good way out. Divorce is so messy—the world pointing at you, learning all the nasty details in court. It's much better being a widow, only how many men are obliging enough to die conveniently? And after one, people would start to talk.

"But you're right about letting her run my life, David." She looked straight at Lenore, and her face reflected the same assurance as the painted portrait behind her. "I'm not a child any longer, mother. I can take care of myself. I can take care of myself just like you."

The real face reflected the painted one, or was it the other way around? *Alike as two peas in a pod,* Flood's voice said in my mind.

"Just like you," Genea repeated.

Lenore said, "I see," and the smoke-and-whiskey voice carried quiet satisfaction.

"Go pack," David said.

Genea shook her head. "There's no need now. Mother and I understand one another, don't we?"

"Yes," Lenore said.

David stared at her. "But I love you. You've said you love me."

Genea frowned. "I don't need it now."

Alike as two peas in a pod. Cold trailed down my spine. I saw a house burning down around a drunken, abusive husband and a fortune hunter crashing a car because fights with a woman destroyed his concentration. A row of death-mask faces lined the walls of the hall. "David," I said, "forget about it. Let's go."

He shook his head. "No!" Disbelief and hurt rang in his voice. "What do you mean you don't need my love now?"

She scowled at him. "Why are you so dense? As long as my mother stops interfering in my life, I don't have to leave here. I don't need anyone to take me away. So I don't need running away; I don't need to be tied to you by emotion; I don't need *you*. You may leave without me."

"Genea, please." Still not believing, David reached for her, and she came around on him with an angry hiss. She struck out at him. She would only have had to knock away his arm, but she went for David himself, hitting him in the chest with stiffened arms.

Caught off balance, David staggered backward into the stair railing, teetered, frantically waving his arms to regain his balance, and fell backward over the railing. Something like the crack of a dry stick sounded through the hall above the music and conversation as he hit the floor.

People screamed. Maybe I did, too. In five seconds, I was down the stairs, elbowing my way desperately through the crowd to David, sprawled on the parquet floor, his hips twisted at an impossible angle to the rest of his trunk.

"My legs," he whispered in terror. "Oh, god, Chris, I can't feel my legs!"

"Someone get a doctor," I pleaded.

I looked up to where Lenore and Genea stood at the top of the stairs. Perhaps it was in blinking back the tears that blurred my vision, but the mode changed, and I found myself seeing them in infrared. In that mode, the sun had gone from Genea. Beside Lenore, their arms around each other like dear friends, they became identical dark shadows peering down at David and me, mirror images radiating cold that ate the heat and light about them. On my knees beside David, touching his anguished face, I shivered as in a wind from a glacier.

Ménage Outré

◦◦◦◦◦◦◦◦◦◦◦◦◦◦◦◦◦◦◦◦◦

AT night, the sound of flutes and drums pulsed across the lawns toward my villa from the miniature castle next door. The high, repetitive melody of the pipe wailed a counterpart to the drum beat, and everything about me felt as if it were resonating to the atavistic rhythm, from the glass walls of my villa to the moon-rimed waters of the Lunamere licking at the cliffs below my terrace. Even my bones reverberated.

I stood on the terrace watching the lights of Aventine shine like stars on the mountainside and staring at the castle. The Radleighs were in Europe for the summer, I knew. Who had leased their house? Lights showed through the draped windows on the lower floor, but I saw no obvious activity inside. The occupants all seemed to be on the crenelated battlements. In the darkness there, they leaped and gyrated in time to the throbbing beat, shadows, black against black. Only one was clearly visible, and that one stood alone, tall and straight, silhouetted against the lemon disc of the rising moon.

"Do you suppose the Radleighs let the house to neopagans?"

My sister Dee moved behind me near the sliding doors from the study. "I don't know."

I turned to look at her. Even here in the darkness, where her awkward nose and jaw were only a blur, she did not look back but kept her head bent, her eyes on her feet.

I frowned. "I was in the study all day finishing the

program for the new novel, but you must have seen them moving in."

The long oval of her face lengthened and foreshortened again as she nodded.

"Who are they?"

"I . . . didn't talk to any of them."

I sighed. No, of course not. Except for me, about the only other person she spoke to face to face was Krista Beck, the girl who helped her keep house. "Can you at least tell me what they look like?"

"There is a woman. She's . . . beautiful." The last word sounded wistful.

I looked back at the figure before the moon. It was distorted now, bent toward the gyrating shadows. Above the flutes and drums, a laugh carried to me. When the figure straightened again, it stood in profile, definitely feminine.

"Well," I said, "there's no time like the present to meet them."

I headed for the hedge dividing the two properties. Dee did not follow, but I had not expected her to. Approaching the castle, I cupped my hands around my mouth. "Hello on the battlements."

Movement stopped with the abruptness of a thrown switch. The tall woman moved along the battlement to step into a crenelation directly above me. "Hello below." It was a rich voice, feminine, with an accent. I tried to place it. Mostly British but mixed with something else.

Around her, the others clustered at all heights. What were they doing, having a costume party? The moonlight outlined some very peculiar shapes, including what looked like plumed and horned helmets.

"I'm your neighbor, Jason Ward."

"Oh, yes, the novelist. Mr. Gordon, the realtor, mentioned you. I'm Simha Barnard. What may I do for you?"

Her name sounded familiar, but I could not remember where I had heard it before. "I thought that as we're living next door to each other, we ought to become acquainted."

There was a pause, then, "Of course. I'll be right down."

She disappeared from the crenelation. The others remained, however, staring down at me and talking among themselves. One of them said, "I hardly think so," in answer to some question I had not heard, and all of them laughed. I had the uncomfortable feeling the question had been about me.

Presently, the great door rolled open. I stepped back, too, involuntarily. In the opening appeared not the woman I had been expecting but the squat shape of a hunchbacked dwarf. His face looked as though the two halves of it had been glued together without being checked for alignment. The higher eye peered up at me, and his mouth produced a twisted diagonal of a smile.

"Come in, please."

I crossed the little drawbridge and stepped under the portcullis through the door. The hunchback shut the door behind me. The echo of it boomed back at us from the distant corners of the great hall.

"This way."

He led in a crab gait that looked awkward but was surprisingly fast. I had to stretch to keep up with him. After the first shock wore off, he amused me. It was appropriate, somehow, to find a miniature Quasimodo in a miniature castle.

The hunchback opened another set of doors. These led into a library where Simha Barnard waited for me before the empty fireplace. It was then, seeing her in the light in a dress-length dashiki, that I recognized her. Dr. Simha Barnard's cosmetisculpturing had made many of the Beautiful People beautiful and kept them that way.

She stood tall and proud, like the aristocratic Masai warriors of her ancestry, with skin like black velvet and hair cropped to a short skullcap. Her eyes were not Masai, though, and I wondered what other blood she carried. They glowed tawny as a panther's in the darkness of her face.

She held out her hand. "I see by your expression

that you know me, but please, don't call me 'doctor.' I'm on holiday."

"I understand." I smiled. "This is an honor, Miss Barnard."

"Simha, please. You seem surprised, too, though I'm sure I don't know why. Does one find anything *but* celebrities in Aventine?" She raised her brows. "Well, what would you like to do to become acquainted?"

The flutes and drums still resonated through the castle. The hunchbacked dwarf remained standing in the doorway. He made no move to leave, and Simha showed no sign of dismissing him. I did not feel like starting an intimate chat under the gaze of those offset eyes.

"I don't want to impose on you too long at this time of night," I said. "Why don't you come for dinner tomorrow evening?"

She smiled. Her tawny eyes focused past me on the hunchback. "Thank you, but this is a rather large household. I couldn't impose all of us on you, and it would be impolite for me to go without them. I have a better idea. Why don't you come here? Mr. Gordon said you have a sister. I believe I saw her peering through the hedge at us earlier. Why don't you bring her, too?"

I blinked. "Dee? But she never goes out."

Simha's brows rose. "Why not?"

"She feels self-conscious about her appearance. She's rather unattractive."

The tawny eyes narrowed. "So unattractive she refuses to go out? Have you ever considered cosmetisculpture for her?"

"Our parents took her to a surgeon once, and he said her bone structure would require extensive work first. It was more than my parents could afford."

"Ah, yes. Well, next to Petit here"—she smiled at the dwarf—"she can feel smashingly good looking, so please bring her. Come at seven and don't dress. We're informal."

I did not relish having a meal with the hunchback grinning at me and Dee trying to keep her head down so no one would see her face, but I did want to know Simha better. "We'll be here."

The hunchback showed me out.

Dee protested in horror when I told her about the invitation. "How could you do that? How can I sit beside a woman like her?"

"Politely. It's rude to refuse this invitation, and it's time you started to meet people. I'm sure Simha doesn't care what you look like."

It was not the last word on the subject, of course. I had to tell her about the hunchback and rant histrionically about having promised our mother I would look after her. In the end, though, her resistance crumbled, and the next evening I was able to drag her through the hedge and across the lawn to the castle with only an occasional whimpered, "Please, Jase," as she trailed after me.

I pretended not to hear. It had been a good day. Not only had I finished programming the computer with the opening scene and all the biographical data on my novel's characters, but the computer had already finished the first chapter that afternoon. Now I was about to enjoy an evening in the company of a beautiful woman.

Inside the portcullis, I pulled at the bell.

The hunchback opened the door. With his high eye aimed at our heads while the low one focused about our knees, his diagonal smile looked like a leer. "Welcome."

Dee started to back away. I caught her wrist and pulled her in after me.

"Everyone has been looking forward to meeting you," the hunchback said.

The "everyone" he referred to were at the far end of the great hall. At first, I thought they were dressed up as they had been the night before, but as I neared them, I realized with a start that they wore no costumes. The odd shapes were their own.

They turned, a dozen of them, no two alike, bodies shrunken or twisted, limbs distorted, skins piebald like a horse's or striped like a tiger's. One man had the burly shoulders and heavy, bossed head of a minotaur.

A woman sprouted a crest of feathers. Another had the scaled, patterned skin of a reptile. A man with sleek green skin bore ears spreading out from the sides of his head like great wings. A dozen pairs of eyes in a dozen bizarre faces fastened on us, gleaming with curiosity and what looked like anticipation.

Simha Barnard rose from the middle of the goblin pack, an ebony goddess draped in clinging gold velvet. "How good of you to be prompt." Her tawny panther's eyes jumped to Dee. "This is your sister? Welcome, Dee. Surely that's a diminutive, but for what—Deanna?"

Dee looked up, then swiftly back at her toes. "No."

I answered for her. "Her name is Dulcinea."

Simha's brows rose. "How lovely. Dulcinea—the ideal of womanhood."

Behind her, the goblin pack nudged each other and grinned.

Not looking up, Dee said bitterly, "It was a mistake. My mother thought I was going to look like her, she told me."

"She told you that?" Simha regarded Dee intently. "How fortunate for you you're *not* like her."

I blinked, and even Dee looked up at that, but before I could ask her the meaning of her comment, Simha turned with regal grace to the pack behind her. "Let me introduce my friends." She pointed at each in turn. "Balmon, Abrasax, Kantu." I recalled last night's remark about neopagans and wondered if it might not be true, after all. "Tree, Seer, Verdis—Feather, Jett, Guran, Nimbus, and Teviva."

From a side doorway, the hunchback said, "Dinner is ready."

Simha stepped between Dee and me. She tucked a hand around my arm and took Dee's. "Shall we go in?"

Simha sat at the head of the long table with one of us on each side of her. The others spread down toward the hunchback at the far end. I found myself next to the snake-skinned woman, Istas. The minotaur, Balmon, sat beside Dee. She slid to the far side of her chair, pulling the arm nearest him tightly against her body, so there would be no chance of touching him. From the corner of my eye, I saw Simha's tawny eyes notice and rest thoughtfully on Dee.

I wondered who was going to serve the dinner. Aside from the hunchback, I had seen no staff. I found out quickly enough. The goblin pack was its own servants. They took turns waiting on each other, a democratic procedure but one that resulted in an endless shuffle to and from the kitchen and a clatter of plates and cutlery accompanied by at least half a dozen simultaneous conversations.

Simha appeared undisturbed by the noise even when the hunchback stumbled and dropped a pile of pewter plates. She merely waited for the ringing to die away, then resumed talking. From time to time, she glanced at Dee and sometimes directed a remark toward her, but Dee's attention remained fixed on her plate. She neither looked up nor reacted except to flinch at an occasional particularly loud sound or laugh.

I sighed. I should never have agreed to bring her. To divert Simha's attention, I asked, "How did you happen to become a surgeon?"

"I wanted to be a sculptor, to create beauty, but none of the usual media satisfied me—too static."

"Even tropic sculpture?"

She nodded. "Even tropes. Then, one day, I heard a woman talking about cosmetisculpture and suddenly realized that flesh is the only truly dynamic medium." She looked down at her hands. The long ebony fingers curled as though grasping a scalpel and osteotome. "So I enrolled in medical school."

"You have your wish, then. You're creating plenty of beauty now. Judging by the pictures of the new Melicenda Hearst, she's a masterpiece, a proud accomplishment for any surgeon."

The words fell into one of those unaccountable lulls in conversation. Along the table, heads turned toward us.

Instead of smiling, however, Simha frowned. Her lip curled. "Hearst is hardly a masterpiece. She's only a potboiler, nothing I can take pride in."

I blinked. "But she's now considered one of the world's most beautiful women."

Simha's nostrils flared. "Since when is a mass-produced commodity beautiful? Hearst and her kind are no better than plastic mannequins. Not one of them has ever come to me and asked to be made beautiful. No, they only want me to make them look like Lillith Mannors or Eden Lyle, or if the patient is a man, like Eric Wayne. They're content to be copies!" Her tawny eyes flashed in scorn. "They're like all these computer-written novels, technically perfect but soulless, made to formula, each exactly like the one before it."

The pack grinned. The piebald man chuckled.

Heat crawled up my neck. "Everyone uses computers to write these days. The critics think very highly of my work."

Her brows rose. "Those same critics also give awards to paintings by chimpanzees."

My mouth tightened. I felt thirteen pairs of glittering eyes burning into me. "Then what *do* you consider beautiful?"

"The rare, of course; the unique." The tawny eyes traveled the length of the table. "These."

These? I struggled to keep myself from staring at the goblin pack in horror. I felt I ought to make some kind of reply, but no words would come.

Simha did not wait for a reply. "Each is unique, one of a kind. As gems are treasured for their rarity, so I value these members of my household, a gallery of the rarest gems of all, collected works and original masterpieces."

Dee lifted her head to follow Simha's gaze incredulously.

Original masterpieces? I slid a covert glance at the minotaur and snake-skinned woman. Surely Simha did not mean what she sounded like. How could someone who created the face Melicenda Hearst wore turn to another human being and produce a monstrosity like one of these?

Simha lifted her brows at me. "I suppose you think they're grotesque?"

I flushed, wishing she would not talk like this in front of them. They watched the both of us with animal intensity. I could almost see their eyes reflect the light, animallike.

"As if grotesque were something shameful," Simha said, smiling at the pack. "It isn't. Like love and hate, the extremes of beauty are simply different sides of the same coin, not opposites. The truly grotesque transcends mere ugliness to become sublime."

The pack applauded.

I became aware that Dee was staring at Simha. The black woman turned with panther grace to smile back; for once, Dee did not look away.

The meal ended. As the minotaur and the piebald man picked up the dishes, Simha said, "Istas and Feather have planned some kind of entertainment. Will you do us the honor of staying for it?"

Her remarks about computer-written novels still rankled. I shook my head. "We can't tonight. I have work to do."

"What a pity. Feather's productions are always so original. Perhaps Dulcinea would like to stay even though you can't." She lifted an inquiring brow at Dee.

Dee looked at me.

"I'm afraid not," I said.

The tawny eyes hooded. "Another time, perhaps. Goodnight. It's been a pleasure to meet you, Dulcinea."

The hunchback showed us to the door. The night air felt cool and blessedly clean. I filled my lungs with it. The door closed with a hollow boom, and inside a flute began to play. I did not stop walking until we had reached the terrace of our villa, as though it were a sanctuary and we could not safely look back until we were on it. Lights flicked on all over the castle.

"That's one invitation I'm sorry I accepted."

Shadows swept back and forth across the windows high in one tower. The flute was joined by drums again. This time, I could hear the heartbeat of Simha Barnard's tribal forefathers in it. The shadows in the tower stretched and distorted as they crossed the lights inside, even more inhuman than the people casting them.

"I wonder what the Radleighs would think if they knew their home had become pandemonium for the summer." They would no doubt think it was kinky fun. I sighed. "I've had enough of demonfolk for one night." I started for my study, then stopped. Dee still looked at the castle. "Dee, are you coming in?"

"Soon."

It was at least an hour, however, and when she did, her homely face carried a faraway look.

The next morning I found her on the terrace twice, staring next door. The first time, there was no sign of activity. The castle could have been deserted. The second time, most of the *outré* household were by the cliffs, laughing and talking while they sunned themselves on the grass, looking for all the world like a flight of demons straight out of medieval art. Two had descended the spidery stairs down the cliff and perched on the rocks below, dangling bare toes in the Luna-mere.

"What are you doing, Dee?"

She shrugged.

Someone called my name. I looked around to see Simha coming through the hedge and across the lawn toward us, wearing only a loincloth. She moved with unself-conscious ease. Putting a hand on the terrace railing, she vaulted it gracefully as a gazelle. "Good morning, Jason—Dulcinea. I owe you an apology for my remarks about computer novels last night. It was shamefully rude of me when you were my guest. I hope you'll forgive me."

Her words still hurt, but I have never been able to resist a beautiful woman. Standing there tall and regal, her skin gleaming in the sunlight, Simha Barnard looked breathtaking. "Of course," I said, and added gallantly, "I should learn not to be so thin-skinned. How was the entertainment?"

On the castle lawn, the feather-crested woman shrieked in laughter.

Simha glanced in her direction, then back at me and

blinked slowly, like a cat. "Oh, quite—creative. How is your novel coming?"

"Well."

In my study, the computer chimed.

"There's the end of chapter five." I started for the doors. "I need to edit now."

Simha nodded good-bye.

I slid the study door closed behind me and scooped the printout from the rack. As I went through it, I could hear snatches of voices from the terrace, Simha's like rich music, my sister's, thin and reedy. Once I glanced out to see them standing together by the railing, looking down over the Lunamere, the dark velvet head bent down to the pale one. She was gone, however, by the time I finished editing and came out for lunch.

The lawn next door was also empty. I glanced toward the castle. "What did you two find to talk about for so long?"

Dee looked up at the peevish tone in my voice, then bent over her plate again. "Just places she's been— people she's known."

It sounded innocent enough. So why did I feel a cool wave, as though a cloud had slid over the sun?

Simha became a regular visitor. Every day she slipped through the hedge and on to the villa's terrace. At first, she came alone. Later, one or two of the goblin pack accompanied her. Her charm made up for her menagerie, however, as she told delightful anecdotes about her travels and acquaintances. But while I was included in the conversation, her eyes always moved past me to Dee, and after Dee began going next door as often as Simha came over, it became painfully obvious that Simha had no interest in me, only in Dee.

That was hard to accept, that she wanted the company of an awkward, shrinking creature like my sister. Dee was only homely, not a freak. What about her was there to interest our odd neighbor?

"Are you enjoying the circus?" I asked Dee as she came back one afternoon.

She bit her lip. "Once you get used to them, they don't look so terrible. You should come with me once in a while."

"I'm trying to finish my novel."

Her eyes widened in surprise and a kind of wondering delight. I winced. Even as I had said it, I realized the remark rang with the jealous overtones of a bruised ego, and Dee had heard.

I began to avoid the terrace when Simha was there. Much as I hate leaving home, it was almost a relief when my agent called.

Leo Carakosta's voice came over the phone line from New York, bouncing with enthusiasm. "I have some autograph sessions set up to kick off the publication of *The Days Like Sand*. It means coming out of your hole, but I think you should. How close are you to finishing the new one?"

"I'm editing the last chapter now. When do you want me there?"

He paused. I pictured him staring at the receiver, wondering that I agreed without even one argument. "Can you possibly catch a plane tomorrow?"

"I'll bring the new manuscript with me."

I hung up and went back to work with a passion. Editing was finished by midafternoon, and by dinner the computer had printed out the complete revised manuscript. Dee came in to find me boxing the printout.

"If you're going to Gateside tomorrow to mail it, will you run some errands for me?" she asked.

I told her about Leo's call.

Her eyes widened. "And you're going?"

"Is that so surprising? I've had autograph sessions before. I've even taken speaking tours. Come see me off at the jetport and you can run your errands yourself."

Her chin ducked. She stared at her feet. "You know I can't do that, Jase," she whispered.

"Then you'll have to send Krista." I paused, then went on. "Don't socialize so much while I'm gone that you make her do all the housework alone."

She tucked her chin tighter. "No, Jase."

*   *   *

The next morning I caught the first cabletrain for Gateside. The morning was clear and sunny, making a spectacular hour's ride suspended above the sheer mountain sides, but my mind kept sliding back to Simha. What could she want with Dee? Maybe I should not be leaving. On the other hand, I would only be gone a week. What could happen in just a week?

Leo met me at the airport in New York and gave me the itinerary as we rode downtown. He had more than "some" autograph sessions; he had ten of them arranged in five cities in as many days. Once the new manuscript had been delivered to the publisher, I became too busy even to think about Dee, let alone speculate on Simha's relationship with her. I signed books in New York, Chicago, St. Louis, Los Angeles, and San Francisco, though the only reason I knew they were different cities was because of the jet rides between. For the rest, the bookstores looked alike, and there was the same blur of faces beyond out-thrust copies of *The Days Like Sand*. My hand wrote automatically: "To Evelyn, to John, to Cassia, best wishes, Jason Ward," with the *J* large and elaborate, its crossed top sweeping on to become the *W*. I smiled until the rictus felt permanent. "Thank you. Yes, this is a lovely city. I'm glad to be here. Thank you. Who would you like it signed to? Will someone get me some coffee, please? Thank you."

Then, as the last session in San Francisco was ending, I recognized a face—gossip columnist Marion Danforth, wearing an impeccable Gucci suit and a sly smile. "Congratulations to your computer. It followed the formula for an adventure plot perfectly. The masses will love it. Tell me, so I can tell my readers, who are always eager for tidbits about celebrities, how do you find the world outside your mountain hideaway?"

I tried to match his smile as I signed the book and reached for another. "I take the cabletrain to Gateside and board a plane. The pilot knows the way."

His smile only became more predatory. "I'm surprised you left home. I understand you have a beautiful new neighbor. You mean you aren't joining the good doctor's gallery?"

I signed another book and returned it without giving conscious thought to the action. "Im no Adonis, but I'm not ugly enough to be a candidate for her collection, either."

"Ah, but she always needs raw material."

I stopped in midsignature to stare at him. "Raw material?"

"Of course." Every syllable dripped malicious delight. "She doesn't carve her monsters from wood, you know."

The words clanged in my head. I scribbled my name in the last copies and pushed away from the table to hunt Leo. "I want to go home now."

He nodded, smiling. "Your flight leaves at ten tomorrow."

"I'm going *tonight*. Get me a cab!"

I left him standing open-mouthed.

I was back in Gateside barely in time for the last cabletrain of the evening. My runabout sat where I had left it at the Aventine station. I jerked the plug out of the charger and vaulted into the car. Its tires clawed at the paving as I gunned it out Callisto Avenue toward home.

The villa was locked and dark. Next door, the castle showed a scattering of lights on its upper floor, but nothing inside moved visibly. I heard no flutes or drums and saw nothing moving on the battlements.

I let myself into the villa with my key. "Dee!" The carpets and drapes swallowed the sound of my voice.

I headed for her room but was not surprised to find it empty. She was probably next door.

I had turned to leave when I noticed the closet standing partially open. Almost reflexively, I pushed it closed—and stopped. The sound of the closing seemed somehow odd, hollow. I jerked the door open again.

The closet was empty! I sucked on my lower lip. No wonder it had sounded hollow.

I reached for her chest of drawers. One after an-

other, I pulled out the drawers. They were empty, too.
The cabinet in Dee's bathroom had been cleaned out,
and the bedside table.

I called Krista. "Where's my sister?"

At the other end of the line, Krista's voice sounded
nervous. "Three days ago some of those—people next
door came and packed her things. They said she was
moving in with them."

"*They* said? Dee didn't tell you herself?"

"I never saw her after that."

I hung up cursing myself for having left Aventine. I
peered around the drapes of a window at the castle. I
should have suspected something like this might happen. Now Dee was trapped over there, brainwashed or
a prisoner. I had to find her and free her before Simha
turned her into another member of the goblin pack.
How did I go about locating her, though? It might be
a small castle, but compared to my villa, the building
was very large. It would be full of people, too.

I pressed my fingers to my temples, straining to
think of a way to get in. Something tickled my mind.
Ah, yes. Just before I left, a landscape service from
Gateside had begun trimming trees and sculpturing
hedges. They had brought a good deal of equipment
the first day and left it because hauling it back and
forth on the cabletrain every day was too much trouble. If I could judge by previous times landscape work
had been done on the castle grounds, it would not be
finished yet. That meant the equipment should still be
here.

I slipped outside and through the hedge, then across
the castle lawn, around the other side of the building.
The castle loomed above me, blotting out the sky. I
found myself glancing repeatedly at the battlements,
afraid I would see demon eyes suddenly glowing there
or a horned head silhouetted against the stars and
hear a shout as I was discovered.

There was nothing, though. All that topped the battlements was the waning moon, touching a tower roof
like the perching of a slender bird. The air carried
only the fresh scent of mountain pine, the sound of

birch leaves rattling like rain in the night breeze, and a woman's voice singing sweet and clear.

I found the landscaper's trailer. A long ladder lay on the ground beside it. I picked up the ladder and swung to regard the castle speculatively. Where would they have put her? Surely not on the side near my villa.

I carried the ladder over to the castle and leaned it against the side next to the first window on the upper floor. I started to climb. The ladder shifted, scraping across the stone. I froze. What seemed like an eternity passed, but no heads appeared against the sky overhead. No voices shouted a challenge.

Presently, I climbed on up until I could see in the window. The room was dark. I could not see details, but it appeared empty. I went back down the ladder and moved to the next window.

That room was occupied by a woman whose skin bore tiger-striped fur the texture of velvet. She sang as she combed her striped mane before the mirror. Her voice was the one I had heard while crossing the lawn.

The next two rooms were dark, too; then the fifth held the minotaur and the green-skinned man. They were talking. I could not hear what they said, but at intervals the minotaur laughed in a window-rattling bellow.

Dee was in the sixth room. She sat on the edge of a huge bed, clutching her robe about her, eyes fixed in a glazed stare. I tried the window. It was unlocked and swung soundlessly inward at a touch. I slid through into the room.

I whispered, "Dee."

She started, gasping, and whirled. "Jase!"

I put my fingers to my lips. "Shhh. I've come to take you home. There's a ladder by the window. If you're quiet, they'll never know you've left until it's too late." I held out my hand to her.

She stared at me. "Why should I leave?" She made no attempt to keep her voice down.

I cringed and listened for any sounds that might indicate some of the pack was coming. "Dee—"

"Dulcinea, Jase. My name is Dulcinea, and I want to be called that."

I wished desperately she would use a lower tone. She never spoke this loud at home. "I know Simha must seem like a person with an exciting, romantic life and that you must feel normal in this menagerie that lives with her, but don't you see that by letting them talk you into joining them, you become part of the sideshow? Not only that, but before she's through, Simha will turn you into something just as bizarre as the rest of them."

Dee lifted her chin. "They didn't talk me into joining them; I begged to come. And Simha is going to give me wings, Jase. I won't be able to fly, of course, but it'll look as though I can." She spread her arms, holding the edges of her robe, and danced across the room with the flaps wide. "I'm going to be beautiful."

I felt ill. "No, Dee, no. You'll—"

She whirled on me. "Call me Dulcinea!"

There was no talking to her. How could I reach her? "She's making you think you want this; it isn't really your idea. Can't you see that she'll make you a freak? People will stare at you more than they ever will with your own face. Please, listen. Stop this madness and come home."

"I *am* home. Home is somewhere you're wanted."

"I want you."

"Do you?" she asked. "Or do you just want a housekeeper?"

"Don't be ridiculous." My voice was rising in exasperation. I forced the tone lower. "I'm your brother. I want to take care of you."

Her laugh was short and bitter. "Because mother asked you to. I don't think you really care anything about me. I think you're indifferent. Simha isn't indifferent."

I wanted to shake her. I made myself say patiently, "Simha only wants to add you to her collection."

Dee shook her head. "You don't know her at all, but even if that were true, it would be caring. It would be enough. It's better to rule in hell than serve in heaven."

Absolutely no talking accomplished anything. I

reached for her and said in a firm voice, "Come home. You'll see things more realistically there."

She screamed. The sound bounced around the room, echoing off the walls, loud and shrill.

"Dee," I hissed, "for god's sake—"

The door burst open. Goblins boiled through to surround me with flashing, angry eyes and hard fingers.

"He's trying to take me away," Dee cried.

They dragged me out of the room onto the gallery and down the stairs into the great hall. Other goblin faces and one pair of tawny panther's eyes stared up at us from below. Dee hurled herself at Simha Barnard. Long ebony arms closed around her.

Simha's eyes burned into me as I was dragged before her. "You're trespassing, Jason. Get out."

"I've come to take my sister home." I tried to shake off the hands holding me, but they clung, inhumanly strong.

"You're not *taking* anyone anywhere, Jason. Dulcinea is free to live anywhere she wishes." Dee was sobbing. Simha stroked her hair. "Anywhere you wish, pet. And you're free to become whatever you like." The tawny eyes met mine. "We'll protect you from him." To me, she said, "You can give up the burden your mother placed on you. We'll take care of Dulcinea now, as we all take care of each other. Let him go."

The hands released me. I rubbed my numb wrists. "But I'm her brother!"

"But we appreciate her. Good-bye, Jason."

The goblin faces turned toward me: twisted, green, striped, piebald, snake-skinned, furred. Goblin eyes fixed intently on me.

"You can't—" I began.

Thirteen goblin bodies stepped toward me, casting warped shadows on the flagstones of the great hall. I retreated.

"Open the door for him, Istas."

The snake-skinned woman ran to do so.

"Dee—"

"Good-bye, Jason!"

At the door, I looked back one last time. Simha still stood with her arm around Dee. The goblin pack clustered about them both. But Dee was no longer crying. Her face looked almost radiant.

Then the door boomed shut between us.

Bête et Noir

°°°°°°°°°°°°°°°°°°°°°°°°

ON gray days, when the clouds hang in heavy, pewter folds and the wind descends cold and sharp as a blade, I think of Brian Eleazar. We stand facing each other in the sand garden, surrounded by the elaborate and alien patterns of rock outcroppings in a score of minerals and dunes of a dozen different-colored sands. The sand underfoot is fine and white as sugar over a deeper layer of red. Across it, between us, a trail of footprints shows scarlet, as though filled with blood.

Gateside was still thawing out from winter when I arrived at the Blue Orion Theatre to join the cast of Zachary Weigand's new play. Leaden clouds shrouded Diana Mountain, hiding the stargate above the city. The wind blowing over the remaining traces of snow and ice left me shivering despite the efforts of my coat, which fluffed itself and clung to me like a frightened cat. For as long as it took me to pay the cab driver and hurry across the sidewalk into the theater, I thought with regret of the movie I had turned down to take this part. The movie was being made in southern Italy, where the sky was almost certainly clear and the sun shining.

As I pushed through the doors into the Blue Orion, a guard came out of his station, ready to turn back anyone who did not belong. "May I help—" He broke off, a smile of recognition spreading across his face. "It's you, Miss Delacour. Mr. Eleazar said you'd be coming. Congratulations on the Tony nomination for

Silent Thunder. I hope you win. Are you going to play Simone in the movie, too?"

I smiled back at him. "If my agent has any influence at all, I will."

"I'll keep my fingers crossed. Before you go in, may I have your autograph?"

He brought a book from his station. I took it and thumbed through looking for a place to sign. I would be in Olympian company, I saw. The pages already carried the signatures of the theater's greatest, personalities like Lillith Mannors, Eden Lyle, Walter Fontaine, and Maya Chaplain. I found a new page and signed it in a precise hand with ornate capitals: Noir Delacour.

It reminded me why I was not in southern Italy. Zach Weigand's name on a script was enough to fill a theater opening night, but when it was accompanied by Brian Eleazar, who had directed in almost every medium and earned himself a shelf of Tonys and Oscars to prove his competence, the play was sure to draw the attention and acclaim of every major critic. *The Sand Garden* had the additional attraction of being a *theatre verité* production. Improvisational and scriptless drama had become very fashionable, but *theatre verité* was the most popular, and it was playing to huge, enthusiastic audiences.

And, of course, I could not overlook the fact that Brian Eleazar had asked me to be Allegra Nightengale.

"He was almost on his knees begging for you, pet," my agent said when he relayed the offer.

However histrionic he sounds, Karol Gardener rarely exaggerates. There was no real agony over which contract to sign, then. It meant a great deal when a director of Brian's stature begged for a particular actress. The producer of the movie had not begged.

I returned the guard's autograph book. "Can you tell me where Mr. Eleazar is?"

"He's on stage with the rest of the cast. Go right on through."

Warmth was seeping back into me. My coat loosened its grip on my arms and chest as the heat soothed and settled it. I could also feel my hair loosening from the hairpins. To the despair of hairdressers everywhere, it has the texture of quicksilver. I did not need a look in the lobby mirrors to know the wind outside had ruined thirty minutes of Raoul's best efforts. I pulled out the hairpins and let the whole pale, slithery mass fall free down my back as I went into the auditorium.

I love theaters. Full ones are best, of course, but I have a special fondness for empty ones. I love to hear the ghosts of a thousand past performances whispering in the musty silence and feel the golden expectation of performances to come.

I listened to the ghosts as I made my way down the sloping aisle toward the stage in the center. Halfway down, though, I switched my attention to the three men standing in the pool of light on stage. Two were familiar. Tommy Sebastian's classic profile and lambs-wool curls looked copied from a Grecian vase —they probably had been. In contrast to Tommy's beauty, Miles Reed's face was so unremarkable it disappeared instantly from memory. He hardly existed as a person off-stage. Miles was a blank canvas on which he painted every role with a new and different brush. I noticed he had shaved his head for this part.

The third man must be Brian Eleazar. He was smaller than I expected, his head reaching barely higher than Tommy's shoulder, but he radiated a presence I felt even from where I stood. Above the turtleneck of his sweater, the craggy irregularity of his face, what the gossip columnists liked to describe as "Lincolnesque," had a compelling magnetism.

I had reached the stage without their noticing me. I made my presence known. "Good afternoon, gentlemen."

They turned. Miles shaded his eyes to peer past the lights. He grinned. "Noir." He came over to offer me a hand up the steps. "Congratulations on the Tony nomination."

Even Miles's voice was subject to change. Last time we met, it had been deep and rich, today sibilant.

Tommy blew me a kiss. "Darling. 'She walks in beauty, like the night.' "

I squeezed Miles's hand in thanks before I let go and looked past him to lift a brow at Tommy. "That's nice, but do you ever learn more than the quotable bits?"

Tommy grinned, unabashed. "That's all it takes to impress most people."

Brian Eleazar nodded to me. "Good afternoon, Miss Delacour." His voice was unexpectedly deep, rumbling up from the depths of his chest.

I smiled at him. "I'm delighted to be here. I've been looking forward to working with you."

I extended my hand. He managed to ignore it, and I pulled back, annoyed and feeling foolish. Brian had once been legend for romancing his leading ladies. That had ended when Pia Fisher became a fixture in his life; apparently, her influence remained even though it had been a year since her death. After a few seconds, amusement at my own reactions overcame the annoyance and disappointment of being held so clearly at a distance. Only then did I discover that Brian's cinnamon-colored eyes were fixed on me with searching intensity.

Before I could examine that expression, he turned away to four chairs in the middle of the stage. "Now that we're all here, shall we begin?"

A thin loose-leaf notebook lay on each chair—our playbooks. I found the one with "Allegra Nightengale" on the cover and sat down. The playbook would not be a script, of course. *Theatre verité* uses no scripts. The notebook contained the biographical history of Allegra Nightengale.

The biography is what makes *theatre verité* unique. Instead of merely adlibbing from an opening situation as in most improvisation or playing roles as in conventional drama, actors in *verité* learn the histories of their characters—absorb them, actually—until they know how the character will think and feel and react to any given situation. Then, with an angel's aid, they *become* the characters. The action of the play emerges from the natural response of the characters to each other.

And because many factors can affect a response—a variation in another's tone or inflection, a distracting sound, the normal day-to-day difference in outlook— no two performances are ever quite alike. Numerous *verité* productions have ends that change from night to night. The dynamic nature of the form, the limitless possibilities in each new performance, are what brings in the audiences.

I opened the playbook. The first page was a scenario of the opening and a tentative outline of the hoped-for action. Authors have some idea what they want to happen. They design their characters to produce personalities that will react in the desired manner. They also hedge their bets by stating their expectations. No matter how involved the actors become in their characters, then, the professional subconscious steers a course in the right general direction toward a satisfactory climax.

"Read over the outline and opening scenario, please," Brian said.

I had examined the outline in Karol Gardener's office when I signed the contract, but I read it again. Brian paced while we did so; on every turn, I felt his cinnamon eyes return to me.

Allegra Nightengale and Jonathan Clay were lovers, the sun, moon, and stars to each other. Jonathan was also a speculator. He had an option to buy a cargo brought back by an exploration team from a planet the stargate touched once and lost. Because the planet had no receiving station, reestablishing contact with it was virtually impossible. That made the cargo priceless. Jonathan went to a Shissahn living on Earth for financial backing. Hakon Chashakananda was a careful businessman and demanded some security to ensure the return of his loan. The opening scenario had Hakon, played by Miles, telling Jonathan, Tommy, to leave Allegra with him as a hostage until the cargo was sold and profits distributed.

I went on to the plot outline. If Zach Weigand had tailored Jonathan's character correctly, Jonathan would agree to the arrangement. Allegra would also agree, out of her love for Jonathan. She would be repelled by the alien because of both his inhuman appearance and his demand for a hostage, but gradually she would find aspects of him to admire. On returning to Jonathan, however, Allegra would find herself looking at him with new eyes. She would find flaws in him she could not accept, and she would leave this once-beloved man of her own kind to return to the alien.

"All right," Brian said. "Study the bios tonight and start learning your characters. Do you all have your angels?"

Miles and I nodded. Tommy shook his head. Brian handed him a vial of minute white pills. "Don't take more than one. I don't want you to settle in too deep. Tomorrow we'll begin scenarios and bio alterations as necessary. I shouldn't need to, but I remind you not to discuss your bios with each other."

We all nodded. We knew not to. Too much knowledge of each other could interfere with the validity of the reactions. We should not know more than the characters naturally would.

"And in the same spirit," Brian went on, "I don't want you socializing with each other off-stage." He looked at all of us, but it seemed to me he stared hardest at Tommy.

We stared back. Not socialize? That was unheard of.

Tommy's eyes rounded in dismay. "Are we supposed to become hermits until the run is over?"

The cinnamon eyes looked through him. "I'm sure you can find friends among the locals."

"But casts usually spend time together off stage on out-of-town runs," Miles said.

"*Theatre verité* is not traditional drama." Brian paced before us like a drill sergeant before his troops. "It's my firm belief that when there's no script to follow and your reactions must all come up out of yourselves, personal relationships inevitably affect those of the characters you're becoming. How can Allegra be repelled by Hakon the first time she meets him if Noir has been Miles's close companion?"

I have sometimes experienced personality bleeding during *verité* productions, so I realized Brian had a point, but I thought his precaution against it was extreme. We were experienced actors, not amateurs, practiced in living with multiple personalities and keeping them separated. What bleeding there might be would not affect the performance noticeably.

Tommy said, "During *Rainbow Man,* Giles Kimner said he thought antagonistic characters should keep their distance off-stage to avoid diluting the hostility, but he had no objections to sympathetic characters mixing, and even with the antagonists he never insisted—"

Brian cut him off coolly. "I'm not Giles Kimner, so I *do* insist that the only contact between you be here in the theater. Our job is to produce *The Sand Garden*, not party. Anyone who cannot live with my direction is free to leave the cast. In fact, I'll insist on it. Is that clear?"

Tommy shrugged. "Youse is da boss, massa." He sighed melodramatically. "I hope I can find a friendly female somewhere in this bleak city to comfort me in my solitude."

"Do you understand?" Brian looked at Miles and me in turn.

Miles nodded. I frowned—I liked Miles and Tommy and had been looking forward to spending free time with them—but I nodded, too. I could always hope Brian would relax his rules later; until then, I needed the time alone to learn who and what Allegra Nightengale was.

"That's all for now. Don't go into the substage until I give you permission to use the sets. I'll see you here ready to work tomorrow morning. Noir, I want you at nine o'clock; Tommy, at ten; and Miles, at eleven. We open in one week."

Tommy groaned. "The thing I hate about working up a play is getting up in the middle of the night to do it."

Brian's cinnamon eyes flicked over Tommy and

passed on. He turned away. As he did, he looked at me one more time. His eyes remained fastened on me even while his body continued turning. He stepped forward beyond the circle of lights and disappeared.

Tommy brightened. "We're free. Anyone for a drink?"

Miles shook his head. "I'm not ready to buck the boss just yet."

"Noir?"

I waved my playbook at him. "Bio, Tommy. Study."

"I'm going to have a drink first." He stood and headed for the steps. "I saw some delectable creatures in the Beta Cygnus Café when I came by on my way here. Perhaps they're still there. *Au revoir.*" He blew us a kiss before he left.

Miles and I sat for a moment longer just looking at each other. "Well, it was nice to see you again, Miles. I don't suppose we'll be doing any practice scenarios since our characters have never met."

Miles stood. "We can at least walk to the door together. That's still in the theater." He offered me his arm down the steps.

I tucked my hand around his elbow. "Isn't Brian overworried about personality bleed?"

My tone was noncommittal, but Miles must have heard the irritation under the words. He said, "Not bleed. It's character carry-over that worries him. Don't you know how Pia Fisher died?"

"I know she drowned."

"It's how she came to drown." We reached the lobby. He stopped beside one of the aquarium benches and looked down through the transparent top at the fish swimming in bright flashes through the water and greenery inside. "Pia was the mermaid in *Rainbow Man* while it was touring in Hawaii. One afternoon, she went out and tried to swim around one of the points along the coast. The trouble was, Pia couldn't swim."

I shuddered at the thought of that lovely young actress so caught up in her mermaid hallucination that she had walked into the ocean. It explained Brian's attitude. We were much more likely to fall into carry-over characterization with each other than around unconnected outsiders.

"Poor Brian. Thank you for telling me." I waved to the guard as we left the theater. "Where are you staying, Miles?"

"The Diana Radisson."

I smiled. "Really? So am I. Much as I want to follow our director's orders, I think it would be a waste to call for two cabs, don't you?"

We shared the one Miles hailed. Despite Brian, we talked all the way to the hotel, catching up on where we had been and doing what with whom since the last time we worked together. I enjoyed every forbidden moment of companionship.

At the hotel, though, we went to our separate rooms. I changed into a comfortable robe and ordered hot tea from room service, then curled up in a chair with the playbook. I am a quick study. I read twice through Zach Weigand's notes on Allegra Nightengale and laid the playbook aside. Then I went to my bag for my angels. I took one.

I can never remember the full chemical name of the angels. They are a derivative of PCP, though. Government research developed it, the story goes, for use in espionage and the witness protection program. With it, spies could assume an undercover identity so completely they could not be blown even under drug or hypno interrogation, and the previous identities of relocated government witnesses would never be betrayed by old habits or mannerisms. The government could not only guarantee a new identity; it could provide a personality to match.

Inevitably, the drug had leaked on to the streets where trippers, ever on the lookout for a new high, gobbled it in high expectation. They were bitterly disappointed. It did not magically turn them into someone else. The angels are only a tool. A new personality requires study while using the drug. So, eventually, the trippers forgot about it, and actors began using it. There is a saying in the theater these days that ordinary productions take one kind of angel, the one with an open checkbook; *verité* needs two angels.

I began to feel the first effects of the angel. My head went light. It seemed I was looking at the room through the wrong end of binoculars and that I heard sound from a great distance.

I lay back in my chair and mentally reread the bio. The words appeared printed across the inside of my eyes. While I read, I tried to visualize the people and scenes the words described. I created faces for Allegra's parents and friends. I built the houses, towns, and schools of her life. I looked at it all as it would be seen through Allegra's eyes and included fine details, right down to the contents of her school locker.

As the images developed, I could feel myself slipping into Allegra. Taking on a new identity is a feeling I enjoy, rather like pulling on a body suit. When I was finished, she would fit me like another skin. The images would be "memories," and she would become "I, Allegra" rather than her present "she, Allegra."

The phone rang. Even at its distance, I recognized the sound as part of the real world. I groped through the angel mist in my mind to reach for the receiver.

Tommy Sebastian's tenor voice sang over the wire with a slight lilt of intoxication. "I'm alone in a golden city with no one to properly appreciate my company. Come relieve my desolation, Noir. 'How do I love thee? Let me count the ways.'"

The sound of my name opened a hole in the angel mist. I became myself. I frowned. "Tommy, you're incorrigible. You heard what Brian said about seeing each other out of the theater."

"We can't possibly see each other. It's far too dark in this bar."

"How did you know where to call me?"

"Elementary, my dear Watson—I called your agent and asked him."

I had to smile. "I'm sorry to put you to so much trouble when I can't accept the invitation. I'm working."

There was a pause; then he said petulantly, "You take old Brian seriously, don't you?"

"I always take my work seriously."

"All work and no play—"

"*No* work makes a poor play," I came back. "Why call me? Surely there are some sweet things who will swoon at the sight of your profile."

"Any number of them, I'm sure, but it's you I want. 'If I were king—ah, love, if I were king— / What tributary nations I would bring / To stoop before your sceptre and to swear / Allegiance to your lips and eyes and hair.' "

I sighed. "Tommy, please go away and let me study."

" 'Had we but world enough, and time / This coyness, lady, were no crime.' You'll miss a terrific evening."

"So I will. Good-bye," I said firmly. "I'll see you tomorrow." I hung up.

I waited a couple of minutes to be sure he was not going to call back; then I let the angel mist wrap around me again and resumed pulling on Allegra's character.

Carry-over let me wear her to the theater. She looked back at me from the mirrored walls of the Blue Orion's practice hall, all pastels and soft focus, dressed in clinging baby blue, hair hanging down her back in a single braid except for the escaping locks that curled in feathery wisps around her well-scrubbed face.

Over the shoulder of the image, I saw Brian appear in the doorway. He regarded me critically, then nodded. "I see you're into her. Take another angel and let's try some scenes."

He opened his playbook and glanced through the notes on Allegra. He chose random incidents from her life prior to the play's opening and played the roles of other people as we acted out the scenes. That is, *he* acted out the scenes; as Allegra, I *lived* them. The practice hall became a schoolroom, my home, an office, and Brian wore the faces of teachers, adolescent loves, and bosses. I, Noir, watched from the back of my head, evaluating my performance. Some of the emotions I felt and words I used, as Allegra, amused me.

Others made me wince. They were not what Noir would have said or felt. They seemed right for Allegra, though.

A little past ten, Brian laid his playbook on the piano and came back to my chair. "That's all for now, Noir."

I shook my head to clear out the angel mist and with a mental somersault to fold Allegra away, resumed being Noir Delacour. "Evaluation, Mr. Director? Criticism? Applause?"

Brian stared at me with an expression so intense I felt as though I were being dissected.

I raised brows at him. "You don't agree with my construction?"

He blinked. "What? I'm sorry; I was thinking of something else for a moment. No, I've no objection. You've made her a warm, loving woman who will certainly do anything for Jonathan and find goodness in Hakon." He smiled. It was a tight gesture, quickly gone.

He had not intended to stare me apart, then; he had just been looking in my direction. I wondered what he had been thinking about. Had something Allegra said reminded him painfully of Pia?

Brian looked past me to the door. "You're late, Tommy."

Tommy sauntered in, yawning, unaffected by the reprimand. "You're lucky I'm here at all. This isn't my best hour of the day."

The cinnamon eyes swept down him. "It should be Jonathan's. What's the matter? Did you leave him in your hotel room?" Brian turned away to get his playbook from the piano.

Tommy sidled over to me. "You missed one of my best performances, sweetheart," he said out of the corner of his mouth in a Bogart accent. "I was super, and it was all wasted on a cocktail waitress who kept her eyes closed the whole time because she thought love should be made in the dark."

I put my finger to my lips. If he was not careful, Brian would hear.

He blithely ignored my warning. "I can't guarantee

a repeat, sweetheart, but why don't we give it a try tonight?"

Brian's back was to us at the piano, but he was facing a row of mirrors. His reflected eyes shifted toward us. He must have heard. I held my breath, waiting for his reaction, but he only regarded Tommy's reflection thoughtfully for a moment, then picked up his playbook and turned back to us.

"Good session, Noir. Let me see you again about one o'clock. If Tommy does as well as you did, we'll set up scenarios for the two of you. See the wardrobe mistress while you have time."

I left them and went exploring the rest of the theater. I found my dressing room and the wardrobe mistress. She took my measurements and promised to have some costumes for me to choose between by tomorrow. Mindful of Brian's warnings, I stayed out of the substage where the sets were being built on lowered sections of the stage carousel. I did go up into the auditorium and watch a gaffer work on an empty raised section, programming one set's walls.

It looked as if it might be the horizon for an exterior. The holographic projection was circular, cutting the corners of the stage, and the section visible to me had the outline of low hills. On my far right was the possible early blocking of a building. The gaffer, wearing a microphone headset, walked in and out across the projection line, consulting a chart in his hand and talking into the mike to his colleagues at the computer in the lighting and projection control booth high on the back side of the theater. Piece by piece, details were added and the scene built on the projection.

More a bas relief than a three-dimensional holo, a theater projection wall has a limited depth and a one-way image. From the inside looking out, it's opaque, but someone outside always perceives the side closest to him as transparent. It gives complete visibility to all members of an audience in the round while providing the set boundaries necessary for the illusion of peering in on private lives. It does cut off actors from the audience, however, which I have always regretted, even though a *verité* cast is supposed to react only to its members.

I walked on around the stage to see the rest of the projection. It was unmistakably an exterior backdrop. Details identified the building as the outside of a house. The hills remained puzzling, though. No grass or flowers grew on them, and the few trees were stark and twisted. Then I realized it must be the sand garden of the title.

Someone called my name. I looked around and found Miles waving to me as he cut across the auditorium toward the stairs to the practice hall. His walk had become a sinuous glide. Miles was wearing Hakon Chashakananda to the theater as I had worn Allegra. He was a bit like the projection wall, adding new details to his characterization each time I saw him. I looked forward to the total Hakon on stage even though Allegra would have to dread it.

My watch said eleven o'clock. Brian did not want me again until one. What should I do with the intervening two hours? I remembered Tommy's mentioning a café down the street. I could pass the time by drinking tea and practicing Allegra on waiters. I could people-watch, too, always an enjoyable pastime in a city like Gateside.

I went after my coat.

At one o'clock, I walked back into the practice hall and found the atmosphere so charged that the tension arced almost visibly among the three men in the room. Tommy sat in a folding wooden chair staring at his nails, while Miles stood over him and Brian paced in front of them with a face hewn from ice-rimed granite. My coat is supposed to be only temperature sensitive, but its fibers stood straight on end, then flattened and clung so tight taking it off was like skinning myself.

Brian saw me. His chin dipped in a brusque nod of greeting.

I peeled the last arm free and dropped the writhing coat on an empty chair. "When does the massacre begin? And do I have to attend?"

The cinnamon eyes blinked. Brian took a few deep breaths. "No massacre," he said. "It's just that we have a small problem with Jonathan, or more to the point, with Mr. Sebastian."

He looked around at Tommy. Tommy's eyes remained fastened on his manicure, but his jaw muscles twitched.

Brian sighed. "Miles, you can go. Thank you. See you tomorrow."

Miles headed for the door, smiling at me in passing. It was a tired product. "Have fun."

Brian resumed pacing. "Tommy is *playing* Jonathan Clay, not *being* Jonathan Clay."

"I'm doing what I always do. Giles Kimner didn't complain in *Rainbow Man.*"

"I'm not Giles Kimner, as I pointed out before." Brian's voice remained even, but every syllable crackled like breaking ice. "I do not believe one can produce valid *theatre verité* by *playing* characters. Jonathan Clay has depth. He has layers of feeling and behavior. If he didn't, Allegra would have realized what he was long ago. He has to be done as more than a veneer over the façade that is Tommy Sebastian."

"I'm doing what I always do." Tommy followed his rising voice until he was standing, glaring down at Brian, only centimeters from the director's face. "You've seen me work before. You know what I do. If you don't like it, why the hell did you come asking me to be Jonathan!" He whirled away and kicked his chair.

The chair collapsed and skidded across the polished floor.

"Very good," Brian said.

I blinked. He sounded delighted.

"I've got you feeling real emotion now. Before you've just played at it, as you've just played at *verité*. You've never bothered to learn how to work with angels, only waited for them to do the job for you. I'll teach you how to use them, though, with Noir's help. You are Jonathan. I want you to be him on stage for the whole world. Noir." He turned and looked at me. "What I'll do is set up scenarios for the two of you, and you'll live as many as necessary for as long as you need to until Jonathan becomes real to you and us."

We swallowed our angels and started to work. After the first hour, I could see why Miles had been exhausted. Even with angels, remaining Allegra and seeing Tommy as Jonathan was an effort when the words and reactions coming from him were all Tommy Sebastian. Though we had never worked together in a *verité* production before, I knew Tommy had done several. I wondered how. I also wondered why Brian wanted him for Jonathan. There were many more gifted actors with profiles as beautiful as Tommy's.

We must have lived fifteen repeats of the party where Jonathan and Allegra first met, and that was only one of seven scenarios Brian had chosen for us. When Brian finally let us quit, it was nearly dark outside. I was too tired even to eat. I took a cab back to my hotel and collapsed into bed.

The next day was a repeat of the previous afternoon. Brian let me take short breaks to choose costumes and be fitted for the alterations while he worked Tommy with Miles, but most of the scenarios were between Jonathan and Allegra. It was wearing, and wearying. I stayed in character for so long I started to feel as if Allegra owned my body and Noir was someone who lived in the back of my head.

The blitz worked, though. In the middle of the afternoon, Tommy visibly changed. I found myself talking to someone unmistakably Jonathan Clay. The easy chatter and poetic quotes disappeared, replaced by warm, adoring eyes that said more than words and lingered on me wherever I went. Finishing the scene, we came out of the angel mist and were actually startled to find Brian present.

He measured us with his eyes, nodding. "He's got it." He grabbed me and danced me across the practice hall. "By jove, I think he's got it!"

I started to pull away. I did not want any man touching me but Jonathan. Moments later, I recognized the carry-over. I grinned sheepishly and relaxed in Brian's arms. "Does he have it, or does it have us, boss?"

Brian did not reply. His head was turned watching our whirling reflections in the mirrors. No, I saw a moment later, not our reflections; he was watching Tommy.

Tommy preened himself, grinning. "You should be dancing me, Brian; I'm the one who's done something marvelous."

Abruptly, Brian let me go. A frown rippled across his forehead. He ran back to Tommy. "No, don't quit; don't lose it again. Let me work with you on some other scenes and we'll zip you into Jonathan once and for all. Thank you, Noir," he called back to me. "We'd never have done it without you. You're through for the day."

I picked up my coat and escaped before he could change his mind. I treated myself to a long walk to clear Allegra and the angel mist from my head. I needed it. I kept finding myself looking in shop windows at dresses that, while beautiful, were not my styles. When I felt like Noir again, I took a cab back to the hotel and soaked in the tub, reading a book. I was debating whether I should bother to dress for the hotel dining room or have room service bring something up when the phone rang.

It was Tommy. "How would you feel about having dinner with me tonight?" His voice came over the wire quietly, without its usual flippancy.

"Has Brian given permission?"

There was a pause. "Of course not, but our characters are supposed to know each other and enjoy each other's company. Please, Allegra?"

I frowned. "Don't try that on me, Tommy Sebastian." Even as I said it, though, I could feel Allegra nudging me, responding to Jonathan's voice. I fought a minute, then gave in. Why not? What was the harm? "Pick me up in half an hour."

He knocked on my door in exactly half an hour. I shook my watch in disbelief. Tommy on time? But he was, and he looked me over with approval. "Lovely." He squeezed my hand as he tucked it under his arm and led me toward the elevators. "I thought we'd eat at The Caverns."

That was fine with me. We chatted while we waited for the elevator, and I noticed that he did not once check his reflection in the mirrored wall. In The Caverns, which was paradoxically on the top floor of the hotel, he continued to be attentive while we sat on a stalagmite-supported bench seat at a stalagmite-supported table beneath dim stalactite lamps.

"Thank you for the dinner," I said as we finished, "even though I had it with Jonathan Clay and not Tommy Sebastian."

Tommy rubbed his forehead. "I'm sorry, but I can't seem to shake him off."

"I can sympathize." I leaned my head against his shoulder. "How did the rest of the afternoon go?"

"More of the same. Well, not quite. Brian made some changes in my—in Jonathan's bio. Then he put me through the hoops with the changes. Would you like to take a walk?"

"I would." We did. Hand in hand, we strolled down Stargate Avenue. The clouds that had been drooping overhead the past two days were gone. Through the clear, crisp night, we could see the towering bulk of Diana Mountain and high on it the lights of the building housing the stargate.

"I always thought there should be a shining arch filled with stars," I said, "not just flat, dull buildings."

Tommy squeezed my hand. "Why, you're a romantic."

I thought about it. "Allegra is."

The stargate and the jetport put Gateside on a crossroads of the galaxy. The avenue was lined with shops whose brightly lighted show windows displayed the products of a hundred worlds. We examined fabrics, gems, art works. In one window stood an intricate painting made by pouring colored sands into the narrow space between two sheets of glass.

I pointed to it. "Isn't that from Shissah?"

Tommy peered at the tag just visible under the edge of the glass. "Yes. Would you like it? I'll come back tomorrow and buy it for you."

I stared at him. "You really *are* stuck in Jonathan's skin, aren't you? Snap out of it, Tommy."

He shook his head like someone dazed. "This is weird. I know I've got just Jonathan's personality, not his money, but for a minute there I was thinking I could write a check for that sand painting no matter what it cost."

I nodded. "There can be a lot of carry-over when the character resonates with your own or when it's the first time or two in deep involvement. What's the matter?"

Tommy was shivering. "I wonder if this is how Pia felt."

"Pia Fisher?"

He leaned his forehead against a window. *"Rainbow Man* was her first part in a *verité* production. If I'd understood then what that meant, I would have made sure she knew what she was doing going into the water."

The skin on my back prickled. "You were with her the day she died?"

He stared broodingly in at a bright collection of fabrics. "I was doing Adoni in the show. We had a free afternoon. I rented a car and talked her into coming for a drive with me. She'd been shut up for days on end, never going anywhere except to the theater, just waiting for Brian to call her during breaks in the movie he was directing in Africa. We stopped for a walk on the beach. She started pulling off her clothes and dared me to a race around the point. I'm not a strong swimmer, so I told her I'd drive around and meet her on the far side." He bit his lip. "She never got there." He turned so his back was slumped against the window. "I didn't know she couldn't swim at all. I never thought to ask her if she knew what she was doing."

Of course he had not. It was not Tommy's nature to question people's actions. He would have waved to her as she waded into the warm Hawaiian ocean, then merrily driven off to meet her on the far side of the point.

"You know," he said, "I feel worse about it now than I ever have before. In fact, I'd almost forgotten about being there until just now."

I took his hand. "You couldn't have known how much of her was carry-over. Come on. We haven't finished our walk."

We were ourselves the rest of the way down the avenue and back. Pia had dissipated the last of the angels' effects. We felt subdued. Not even Tommy could find his usual light humor. When we reached the hotel, he left me in the lobby without once extolling his virtues as a night-long guest.

The next day, he came to the theater still quieter than usual. I wondered if I should be concerned, but Brian was obviously pleased. "Jonathan is coming very well. Tommy, I want you and Miles to work together this morning. You'll have to work alone—I have some errands to run—but I think you're capable of it now. Do some early meetings between Jonathan and Hakon."

Tommy's eyes followed me. "Can't I work with Noir?"

"Later. Here comes Miles." He repeated his instructions to the other actor, then picked up his coat and started for the door. "Noir, will you walk to the street with me, please?"

Leaving, I saw Tommy's face. He frowned in displeasure.

Brian walked fast. I had to stretch my legs to keep up. "Is there something you want me to do?"

"Yes. Button your coat and come with me."

I raised brows at him. "What?"

"I have business in Aventine. You've been working hard and deserve a little bit of holiday." His hand closed on my elbow, urging me forward. "A cable-train leaves from here in fifteen minutes. We just have time to make it if we hurry."

I stopped. I would love to see Aventine. That retreat of the rich and famous was legendary, but—by cabletrain?

He pulled me forward again. "It's so high you'll lose the sensation of height, I promise you. You'll enjoy the trip."

I let him drag me along. "How did you know I'm afraid of heights?"

He shrugged. "I suppose I heard it somewhere. Come on."

Aventine. The name had a magic ring. Why not? "All right."

The hour's ride on the cabletrain was not as bad as I feared. With Brian holding tight to my hand, I allowed myself to be talked into looking out the windows. The mountainside fell away hundreds of meters below us, a patchwork of melting snow and new spring green. As Brian promised, as in a plane, there was no sensation of being *up*. The scene could have been a projection wall mere centimeters below the bottom of the train. Brian offered to take me up to the observation platform where coin-operated binoculars let passengers who care to take a close look at the bear fishing in the streams below and the deer grazing in the meadows. I declined. The sway of the train was enough to remind me we were suspended over this chasm on just a cable. I felt more secure sitting down.

"What do you have to do in Aventine?" I asked.

"Pick up a prop. Jonathan is a wealthy man with impeccable taste in women and possessions. I thought we should have some first-class art for his office. Xhosar Kain is creating a sonic sculpture just for the play."

Xhosar Kain? I was impressed. "You're going after it yourself?"

"Would you trust a Kain piece to a delivery service?"

The conversation lapsed for a few minutes. I peeped out the window again. Clouds were starting to move in, some so low they floated under the train. I hoped that did not mean the ride back would be minus the scenery. I felt Brian's eyes on me, measuring, searching. What was it he was looking for in me?

"What are you doing with your evenings?" he asked.

I could not stop the sudden guilty flush that spread up my neck. "Reading, mostly."

"Not going out with Tommy?"

He knew. His voice was neither accusing nor judgmental, but it was clear the question was rhetorical.

"I did last night." I saw no point in denying it. I looked at him. "Why shouldn't we? Jonathan and Allegra are lovers. Our togetherness off-stage should strengthen the bond on stage."

The cinnamon eyes focused past me. "Were you Allegra and Jonathan last night?"

I wished I could read him. I could not guess how far he intended the question to go. "I reacted to him a bit as Allegra while he was very much Jonathan. He had trouble getting out of the character. He went to his own hotel for the night, however."

I wondered for a moment if the brilliant flash in his eyes was anger, but then his face lighted in a smile of satisfaction. "We may make a real actor of him yet."

Minutes later, the cabletrain pulled into the Aventine station. I climbed out rubbernecking with unashamed curiosity. I found the retreats of the rich and famous not immediately visible, however. The station sat at the edge of a shopping square. Off it lay streets with apartments and studios. Long ago, Aventine had begun as an artists' colony, and that still dominated its center.

Brian led the way up one of the artists' streets. He stopped at a sculpture, an "X" elaborately wrought in sonic vanes. The wind set it vibrating in a pleasant if repetitious pattern of chords. Brian pushed open the door of the studio behind it.

I am not sure what I expected Xhosar Kain to look like, a bearlike blacksmith, perhaps. I did not expect the thin man who put down his welding torch and mask to come slowly to meet us. The body looked frail, its spine twisted, but the hand that took mine was large and strong, and his eyes looked warmly into mine.

"Noir Delacour. I'm a great fan of yours."

"And I of you. I saw *I, the Living* when it was on exhibit in New York and felt like I'd had a religious experience."

He grinned. "You are obviously a woman of outstanding judgment. I'll love you to my death." He looked at Brian. "Come after the lady, have you, Eleazar?"

Brian nodded.

"Just a minute."

He limped into the depths of the studio and came back carrying a small sculpture. Once he set it down, I could see it was not at all that small, but it was still less massive than most of his work. It was right for a table or desk.

"I call her *The Fury*. Is she what you had in mind?"

I could see why he called the sculpture "she." My first reaction was that it was a bird with wings spread to fly, but it could also have been a woman. The rising vanes looked as much like flowing sleeves as wings. The piece was beautiful and at the same time somehow frightening. Air currents in the studio set off in it a sound that was now a hum and now a keening wail.

Brian touched the edge of a vane with a tentative finger. "It's just right."

Kain wrapped the sculpture carefully and laid it in a box. He gave the box to Brian. "Watch out for her."

He followed us to the door of the studio. "Come back and let me do a sonic of you one day, Miss Delacour. It will sing as fair as the angels."

I promised I would.

Outside, the sky was still lowering. Leaden, waterlogged clouds rolled across the blue, cutting off the sun. The wind rose, too, setting off discords in the sculpture in front of the studio. My coat fluffed and tightened around me.

Brian looked up. "It's no day for sightseeing, after all. Let's go back to the station."

The weather changed his mood entirely. Eating lunch at the Gallery Café in Aventine while we waited for the next train and during the ride back, Brian sat silent, lost in thoughts that looked as brooding as the sky outside. From time to time, his cinnamon eyes rested on me or the carton he carried, but for the most part he looked past me, focused on some bleak otherwhere. We were back in the Blue Orion before he could shake free of the mood.

He gave me an apologetic smile. "I'm sorry I was such poor company."

I shrugged. "That's all right."

He opened the door of the practice hall. Miles and Tommy stood by the piano drinking coffee. They looked around.

"We're back." Brian forced a gay, almost playful tone into his voice. "Thank you for coming with me, Noir." He kissed me full on the mouth.

Tommy set down his coffee. His eyes traveled from Brian to me. "You went somewhere together?"

"Aventine—to get this." Brian opened the box and took out *The Fury*. "I'll show you where it goes."

He led us into the substage area. Sections of the carousel were dressed, waiting to be turned to position beneath the stage opening and raised into place. Light fell from the auditorium through the stage opening. Three sections remained in shadow. The lighted section was an interior. It looked oddly naked without the projection wall that would be around it when it was in place up top. Brian stepped up on to the platform and placed *The Fury* on a massive desk there.

"This is Jonathan's office. Starting tomorrow, we'll send the sets up top in turn and let you work on them. I want you to thoroughly familiarize yourselves with those you need to know. For you, Noir, that means this office. You still need to keep away from the sand garden and the interior set of Hakon's house. How did the scenes go this morning, Miles, Tommy?"

Tommy's forehead creased. "Why did you go to Aventine with him?" he asked me.

I looked quickly at him. His voice had a note I had never heard in it before, a hard, controlled evenness. I frowned. "That's hardly your concern, but Brian asked me along."

"The period of mourning is over, then, Brian?"

Brian did not respond.

I rolled my eyes. "Really. It was hardly an assignation."

Tommy stepped toward me, his fist clenched. My heart leaped in my throat. For a moment, I thought he was going to raise it to strike.

"Tommy!" Fear sharpened my voice. "Stop that! Tommy Sebastian doesn't care where Noir Delacour goes or with whom. You're letting Jonathan keep too tight a hold on you. Shake him off."

Tommy's mouth opened and closed several times without letting out a sound. He shook his head hard. After a bit, his fist relaxed. "God, I don't know if I can take this." He whirled away and ran out.

Miles went after him. "I'll see if I can help him."

I leaned against Jonathan's desk and sighed. "You may make Tommy a good *verité* actor, Brian, but you're also making him an unhappy, confused human being."

"He's doing beautifully, just beautifully." Brian looked in the direction Tommy had gone, a fierce joy in his cinnamon eyes.

I bit my lip. "Do you really want Jonathan acting like that? It isn't how he usually is around Allegra."

His eyes came around to me. "That's because she's always been so completely, faithfully his. When he finds her admiring Hakon, though, and enjoying the alien's company, it will bring out a side of his character she has never seen before. Sit down, will you? I was thinking about Allegra on the way back from Aventine, and I've decided I'm not quite satisfied with her. I think we need to make a change in her bio."

My brows went up. "Now? We open in just three days."

"That's time enough to incorporate the change. We need a dissonant element in her early life. Up to now, she has always been loved. She's had no reason to distrust anyone. I think she'll work more effectively if there's an element of fear as well as loathing in her initial reaction to Hakon. Let's say that her father died when she was eight and her mother met a man that loneliness caused her to think she loved. The man, though, proved to be very jealous and possessive, and one night he accused Allegra's mother of seeing someone else. He struck her in his rage. She broke off with him and soon afterward married a man who became a gentle, loving stepfather to Allegra."

My skin pimpled. I shivered.

Brian cocked his head. "What's wrong?"

I pulled my braid over my shoulder and toyed with the end. "Something very much like that happened to me. I was ten and my mother divorced, not widowed, but—didn't you know that?"

The cinnamon eyes flickered. "No. Why should I?"

"You knew about my fear of heights."

"That was just chance. I didn't know anything about this." He sighed. "That's going to make it very painful for you, isn't it?"

He had known. I felt it with chilling certainty. He was lying. Why? "Can't we introduce someone unpleasant into her life another way?"

He thought, rubbing his chin. "I wish we could, but I'm sorry. I have to have it this way to achieve exactly the effect I need. If it helps, we won't work through a scenario. You find a name for the man and a way for Allegra's mother to have met him. Just visualize the rage scene and include it in Allegra's memories. All right?"

He said it as though he were offering a concession. I started to protest, to refuse, but his eyes caught mine, steady and compelling. Without ever meaning to, I found myself nodding agreement.

He patted my shoulder. "Good girl. Well, I think I'll see if I can find Tommy and Miles."

I could have left the substage with him, but I stayed, somehow reluctant to step out of the light slanting down through the opening above and into the darkness of the cavernous room around me. I sat down in the big chair behind Jonathan's desk and stared at *The Fury,* trying to sort out my emotions. I could see the face of my mother's lover before me, ugly and inhuman in its rage. I felt again the force of his slap when I tried to pull him away from my mother. And I saw him crumple as my mother struck him with a lamp. I could also see Brian's cinnamon eyes, flickering past me when he denied knowing about that incident in my past. Later, though, he had looked into me with unwavering directness. It shook my conviction that he had known. Perhaps, after all,

he had just chanced to hear about my fear of heights
and it was coincidence that he gave Allegra one moment of history in common with me. Perhaps he did
need just that incident to create dramatic conflict in
Allegra's character.

I started looking around the office. It was so like
Jonathan, all flashy chrome pole lamps and chrome-
framed designer chairs—expensive, handsome, sterile. In it, *The Fury* stood as the single spot of life and
emotion. I leaned across the desk to touch a sonic
vane. The motion stirred the air and set the sculpture
keening. The sound plucked at my nerves. It was like
a wail of grief, sharp and unrelenting. It carried after
me out of the substage and followed me all the way
back to the practice hall.

The last three days before the opening were hectic.
The costumes were ready, and Tommy and I wore
ours while we practiced in Jonathan's office. Miles
disappeared. I hardly came across him except when
coming and going. The one time I saw him long
enough to ask about his costumes, he only laughed
in a long, sibilant hiss and winked.

"It's more of a body makeup. You'll like it. It's
spectacular."

Tommy and I learned to know the office so well we
could cross it in the dark. I came to recognize the feel
of every piece of furniture, the location of every holographic book in the projection wall bookcases.
Tommy seemed to have recovered from his upset the
day I went to Aventine. He was a gentle Jonathan on
the set and almost his old self off-stage, only a little
subdued by his character's *persona*.

We all developed first-night nerves. In a sense,
every night of the run would be an opening night, but
we were products enough of conventional drama to
find something special in the very first night. Also, in
spite of the practice scenarios, we could still not pre-
dict exactly how the characters would react. The
course and end of the play were no certainty. The
agony of anticipation became almost unbearable.

"Think about Zach Weigand," Brian said the afternoon of the opening. "He's going to be in the audience tonight chewing his knuckles wondering if we'll dispose as he has proposed. He's much more nervous than any of you." He herded us toward the door. "Go rest or meditate, whatever you need to be at your best. Be back by seven at the latest. The stage goes up at eight."

I took a cab back to the hotel. I always think I'm going to take a nap before an opening or lose myself in a light novel. I had the book ready. But I ended up doing what I always do. I paced, nerves singing like high-tension wires. I fought to keep from biting my manicure into ruin. Inevitably, I picked up the phone and called Karol Gardener.

His voice laughed back at me over the wire. "Very good, pet. You held out fifteen minutes longer than usual. I have a drink in my hand. I raise it in a toast to you."

I kept pacing, taking the phone with me, phone in one hand, receiver in the other. "You'd think I'd learn to have more faith in myself, wouldn't you, but here I am lost once more in the dreadful broody 'what ifs.' Tell me I'm not going to lay an egg."

"My darling Noir, there is no way in this glorious galaxy you can lay an egg. You'll be superb as Allegra Nightengale. Remember, Brian wanted you and no one else for the part. Do you doubt Brian Eleazar's judgment?"

I stopped, feeling suddenly cold. "Wanted me and *no* one else? Where did you hear that?"

"Prying into the affairs of other agents, pet. Vonda King and Maya Chaplain had their agents wooing him for weeks, but after he had asked around, Brian came after you. He wouldn't hear of anyone else."

Why did that disturb me so? "Asked around where?"

"Well, he talked to Charlotte DeMetro for one."

Charlotte DeMetro? Why would a director talk to a gossip columnist when he was looking for someone to take a character? *Because,* a small voice in me whispered, *gossip columnists know things like who has what phobias and what kind of family histories.* Charlotte knew more skeletons than any other five columnists put together. Why should gossip be important in finding an actress, though?

I did not have time to think more about it. Karol chattered on, giving encouragement and relaying inconsequential gossip. The words ran through my head in a murmuring stream, sound with just enough sense to distract and calm me. My answers could not have been much more than monosyllables, but Karol read them with precision. He knew to the second when my stomach stopped churning and my pessimism lifted, but the keen edge remained on my nerves. That was the moment he broke off.

"You need to get ready to go now. Break a leg, pet. I'll call you tomorrow and see how it went."

He sent me off to the theater at a peak of emotion. I considered asking Brian what he had talked about with Charlotte but did not have the chance. I did not see him until a few minutes before eight and then only as he stuck his head into my dressing room to warn me about the time. His face was shuttered, and his cinnamon eyes focused on otherwhere. I had taken my angels and was busy slipping into Allegra and the first costume. It was the wrong time to ask anything. I shrugged. The question would keep until afterward.

The lights went down in the auditorium and up on the stage. The first scene was between Jonathan and Hakon. I waited in the substage.

The scene ended, and the stage was lowered. Above, I knew, the projection wall would have gone completely opaque and become a swirling storm of opalescent colors. The stage reached floor level. With a smooth hum of motors, the carousel revolved, bringing Jonathan's office into position. Tommy leaped from the first set to the office. A stage hand helped me up on to the platform. Slowly, the stage began to rise. We went up into light, where the audience was a warm animal smell and a sigh of collected breathing beyond the opalescent projection walls.

The sound of the audience retreated to a great distance, beyond the angel mist. I looked at Tommy—Jonathan.

The walls resolved into windows, paneling, and bookcases. I looked at the dearest man in the world and saw he was in pain. My heart went out to him. "Jonathan, what's the matter?"

I, Noir, retreated to the back of my head. From there I watched Allegra critically but without interfering except for a nudge here and there to keep the action and dialogue dramatically interesting.

The action went very much as Zách Weigand outlined in the playbook. As Allegra, I was distressed and horrified by what Jonathan had let Hakon force on him.

"How could you agree to it, Jonathan? It's—barbaric."

Jonathan slumped in his chair, a picture of misery. "He tricked me. I was committed to handling the cargo before I knew the Shissahn's conditions. God, if I'd known what he was going to demand, I'd have cut off my arm first. I'd have let the Corbreen syndicate take the option."

I could not stand to see him in misery. I threw myself at his knees. "It's all right. I'll go."

The walls went opalescent. Jonathan's office sank into the substage. The next set rose. I found myself in the Shissahn's sand garden. Allegra was horrified by it. It was desert, desolation, nothing but rock and sand, no plant life but an occasional cactus or Joshua tree. Noir was entranced. I had never seen anything like it before. I hoped real Shissahn gardens were like it. The rock outcroppings were of many varieties, too many to occur naturally. They gleamed with veins of gold and silver, glittered with crystal and semipolished gems. They studded dunes composed of a dozen colored sands. The main section of the set was a double layer of sand, heavy red under fine silver-white. Mixed together, they made a shimmering pink, then slowly separated into two distinct layers again. Walking across the sand, my feet sank through the top sand to reveal the red beneath and leave scarlet prints that remained a few minutes, bright in the white sand, then disappeared as the top sand sifted into the depression.

The projection wall made the set look as if it stretched for acres.

I was standing in that miniature wilderness working up the courage to go to the house when I heard a sound behind me. I turned and screamed. The creature standing on the top of the dune looked generally humanoid, but it was hairless and earless. Its mottled green, brown, and slate-gray hide had the texture of old leather. A leather kilt wrapped its hips, and a long curved knife hung diagonally across its chest.

"You are the Clay female?" Its voice was the dry hiss of sliding sand. "I am Hakon Chashakananda."

Miles had been right. I loved his makeup. It was spectacular. If I had not known for certain it was Miles, I would have sworn a genuine Shissahn had been rung in for the part.

I backed away, clutching my suitcase, then stopped and forced myself to stand, chin lifted high. I would not run from this creature no matter how fearsome he looked. "I am Allegra Nightengale." I tried to keep my voice from trembling. "Be so good as to direct me to my room."

Friendship with Hakon came slowly. It developed through the next scenes, beginning with impertinent questions: "Why does a supposedly civilized being run around in nothing but a leather loincloth and that hideous knife?" Hakon had his reasons, which he gave me, but in deference to me, he began wearing loose caftanlike robes. Then came curious questions: "What does your name mean in your language?"

His answer began with an almost human grin. "It has no meaning. You could not pronounce my actual name. Hakon Chashakananda is what I have adopted for the benefit of your people."

I blinked. "Then why not use a simple name?"

He blinked, too, in a slow saurian gesture. "What? Would you have an alien named John Smith? Humans expect us to have long and difficult names."

That broke the ice forever. From there, the relationship grew quickly. The I that was Allegra began to see the beauty in the sand garden and the equally fine qualities in the garden's owner.

Soon after that, he sent me home to Jonathan.

Jonathan was startled but overjoyed. He hugged me until I thought my ribs would crack. "How did you do it? I'd have thought he was impossible to move."

"You just haven't had a chance to know Hakon well enough. Today he said, 'I have come to know you well and find you a person of trustworthiness. If you say your Jonathan is a man of honor, I believe he must be. Then I do not need a hostage.' And he let me go."

Jonathan drew back, frowning. "What did he mean, he's come to know you well?"

Inside the angel mist, Noir started. Tommy had used that tone asking why I had gone to Aventine with Brian. Allegra did not hear the change in voice. "We've spent a great deal of time together in four months. I couldn't very well sit in my room alone day after day. I'd have gone mad. It's exhausting to hate, so we became friends. He's really a very fine man."

Jonathan's eyes narrowed. *"Man?"*

I nodded. "Any intelligent being is a man. That's what his people believe. Isn't that a fine concept? It binds us together instead of separating us into alien and human, Terran and Shissahn."

"Have you adopted Shissahn philosophy and discarded human beliefs, then?"

There was no mistaking the displeasure in that question. Allegra reached out to touch his hand. "Of course not, but they do have some ideas worth considering. Are you disturbed by that?"

The muscles in his jaw twitched. "What do you think? I've spent four months in hell, working as hard as I could to sell off the cargo so I could redeem you. I was scared to death for you. I didn't have any idea what that creature might be capable of doing. Now you come back singing his praises and spouting alien philosophy. Exactly how friendly have you been with him?"

His implied accusation shocked me. "He's never touched me. You are my beloved, Jonathan. I've been faithful to you."

He hugged me fiercely. "Thank god. And now we're back together again, we can forget this whole incident and continue where we left off."

We did not, of course. I had been changed by the months with Hakon. I looked at Jonathan through eyes grown a bit alien. I saw things in him I had never seen before, things that deeply disturbed me. When I realized Jonathan was preparing to cheat Hakon out of part of the profit due him, I had to speak out.

Jonathan was brusque. "This is none of your concern."

"It *is*. I promised Hakon you were trustworthy. It isn't right for you to do this."

His anger was not the flaming kind. Outwardly, he remained calm. His voice stayed level, his face clear, but the muscles twitched in his jaw as I talked, and his voice took on the tightness of careful control. He refused to discuss his business and ordered me out of the office.

I looked at him in great sorrow. I had been afraid it might come to this. "Very well. I'll go pack."

"Pack?" He was on his feet. "What do you mean, pack?"

"I'm leaving you."

He came flying around the desk. "No. You can't."

I felt as if I were being torn apart, but I refused to yield to him. I tried to explain how different I felt about things now, how different I saw. He could not understand.

"I knew there was something between you and that alien."

I shook my head emphatically. "You're wrong. Perhaps there could have been, but I remained faithful to you, and he respected my choice."

"Is that so?" His voice rose. "You think he's a wonderful *man*. You bargain on his behalf in business matters that are none of your concern—bargain against *me*, the man you claim to love. Now you want to leave me. And you expect me to believe it isn't to go back to *him*?"

"I expect you to believe that, yes."

"You're lying." He said it through clenched teeth. His hands flexed.

Panic went through me in an icy wash. He was going to hit me! I backed away, feeling helpless and eight years old.

One of his hands drew back, open, poised for a slap. "You're lying to me. Don't you dare do that! Admit there was something between you and the alien. Admit it!"

"No, Jonathan." I tried to back farther, but the desk, that huge, solid desk, blocked my retreat. "There was nothing! I swear it!"

In the back of my head, Noir was screaming. Jonathan wore the face of my mother's lover. The hand swung forward. Allegra groped behind her. I needed something to fend him off. My hand closed on the base of the Kain sculpture.

Noir protested, struggling against the angel mist inside me. The play was not supposed to go this way. Allegra should drop the sculpture, should let him hit me once if necessary and reason lovingly with him. Once I might have, but now Jonathan's hand headed toward my face, and the terrifying memory of another hand and another man paralyzed me. Noir Delacour should have resumed control, but that same image held me snarled in the angel mist. I swung the sculpture at him.

It slashed across his face. The vanes were like dozens of knives, cutting and tearing through cheeks and nose and eyes. Somewhere beyond the walls of the office, there was a shriek and the sharp stench of sweat and fear. Jonathan screamed and clawed for me. I swung the sculpture again. This time, it crossed his throat.

As he went down, I realized what I was doing. I dropped the sculpture and fell on my knees beside him. I tried to stop the bleeding with my hands.

"Jonathan, Jonathan, why did you do this to me? I never wanted to hurt you. I loved you."

Through the angel mist, Noir watched with dull horror and realized it *was* supposed to happen this way. It had been orchestrated. Brian had chosen me for Allegra because of my mother's lover. It was to keep me from stopping Allegra's panic reaction to Jonathan's anger. I was not the only one chosen, though. Brian had asked Tommy to be Jonathan—poor foolish, irresponsible Tommy. Brian had commissioned the Kain sculpture, so appropriately named after those Grecian instruments of revenge.

Allegra cried, "What are we? I found humanity and compassion in an alien and monstrosity in my beloved. Even I, for all my pride in being gentle and civilized, become a clawing animal at the first threat of attack."

Beyond the projection wall, the crowd murmured in excitement. The sound came through the angel mist. My head cleared. I looked down at Tommy, who lay slack and still.

The blood delighted the crowd. Suddenly, I understood them as I never had before. This was why they loved *verité,* what they really came hoping for—modern Romans at a modern circus.

I looked at my hands, red with Tommy's blood. "Who are the men, Jonathan, and who the beasts and aliens?"

I huddled over him. I did not look up when the projection wall was shut off. I would not stand to take a bow. Someone picked me up. It was Miles. He kept an arm around me, holding me against his leathery chest while the crowd screamed its pleasure and the stage carried us down out of their sight.

Miles helped me off the stage in the substage area.

Brian pushed through the crowd of gaffers and stagehands to us. "Noir, how terrible, but don't worry. I'm sure the inquest will find it was an accident, death by misadventure."

I looked around at him, not letting go of Miles. "What a pity," I said bitterly. "Then you can't take proper credit for the most brilliant directing of your career."

He stared at me one flicker of time, then patted my shoulder. "Poor Noir. You're upset."

"What does that matter? Pia is avenged, and that's what it's all been about, isn't it?"

"You'd better take her to her dressing room to lie down, Miles. I'll call a doctor."

I let Miles lead me away, but in the doorway I stopped and looked back. Brian had picked up *The Fury* from where I dropped it and stood holding the sculpture. The light slanting down from the auditorium reflected off the vanes on to his face. It caught his eyes, and as he lifted his head to look back at me, the cinnamon eyes glowed red, like an animal's by firelight.

On gray days, when the clouds hang in heavy, pewter folds and the wind descends cold and sharp as a blade, I think of Brian Eleazar. We stand facing each other in the sand garden, and between us lies a trail of footprints, scarlet in the fine, white sand, as though it was filled with blood.

About the Author

LEE KILLOUGH is a tall redhead who sometimes feels that it was inevitable that she write science fiction. As the daughter of a newspaperwoman and a high school Spanish/English teacher, she grew up with words and the fascination of creating stories. As chief technologist in the Department of Radiology of the Kansas State University College of Veterinary Medicine, her days are filled with the problems of strange and nonhuman species.

She had never considered writing professionally, however, until meeting Pat Killough while in school at Fort Hays, Kansas State College. He encouraged her to begin submitting for publication, and since the appearance of her first short story "Caveat Emptor" in *Analog* in 1970, has been not only chief critic and cheerleader for her writing efforts but also live-in lawyer and business manager. Her first novel, *A Voice Out of Ramah,* was published in 1979. Pat also first introduced her to science-fiction conventions and fandom. She and Pat attend conventions when their work schedules permit. At home, in Manhattan, Kansas, they share a hillside redwood house with a proliferating library and a highly autonomous Burmese cat named Phaedra.

DEL REY BOOKS invites you to enjoy more of the wonderful world of **Oz**